The SONG WALKER

ZILLAH BETHELL

USBORNE

First Country Australian and Torres Strait Islander readers are warned that the following story may contain the names of deceased persons.

This book is dedicated to the Alyawarre community of the Northern Territory.

The author and the publishers thank the Alyawarre community for reading the book and allowing their name to be used.

GLOSSARY OF ALYAWARRE TERMS

ampe – child

anatye – bush potatoes

angente – mirage

aperle – father's mother

arelhe – woman

arrpwere – magpie

atyemeye – mother's father

atyeye – little sister / brother

aywaye – old man

aywerte – spinifex grass

gnamma – waterhole

gwardar – a highly venomous snake

ipmenhe – mother's mother

irntirte – horrible

kele – done/okay/finished

kwarte – egg

kwepalpale – bellbird

tidda – best female friend

werte – hello

yaye – older sister

*Only the song through the land
hallows and heals.*
Sonnets to Orpheus (Rainer Maria Rilke)

Coda – *Music*

The concluding passage of a piece or movement.

(Oxford English Dictionary)

......*right, left, right...left...... right.........left...............right......left.................. right...............................*

Le...ft.

I stop walking.

I didn't even know I was walking until a moment ago but...

I stop.

Still.

Quiet, until I can hear my dry breath.

I don't know where I am. I look around. A red landscape of dust. Flat. Stretching everywhere. And above, a blue, blue sky.

What am I doing here?

My foot is hurting.

The left one.

It is the pain that has made me stop walking, I think.

I look down at my feet. On my right foot I have a black, shiny leather shoe. Pointed at the front. Delicate stitching around the seam. The leather looks scratched and scuffed and dirty. A piece of it hangs off the side of the shoe, dangling like the last leaf off a tree. Underneath I can see the white of the lining, filthy now with red dust.

I look at my left foot.

It is bare.

I lift it and try to see its bottom side. Slivers of small sharp stones stick into the sole, dried earth clumped between my toes. And on the parts of the foot that touch the ground more often than the others – huge blisters. Bulbous, bursting and bloody. Open wide sores with ripped strips of skin. It is no wonder it hurts.

I suddenly feel sick.

I *want to be* sick.

I brush the stones from out of my foot – making the pain even worse for a second – and crash forward onto the ground. The thing I am holding bangs hard on the grit and I let go of its handle.

Lying on the ground I take deep breaths. I close my eyes and imagine…well, I don't know what. Not this, I suppose. I imagine something that isn't this. Something else. Something better.

Something soft and cool and shapeless that I can't quite picture.

That makes the sick feeling go away. Eventually.

So, I open my eyes, roll onto my back and look up at the sky.

So blue.

Like the sea.

I imagine myself in the air – the whole world upside down – as I fall towards this sky sea. The wind rushing itself around my arms and my legs. The birds watching me in awe. Dropping wonderfully towards the water and never splashing into it.

But my body stops me hiding in this dream.

My body doesn't *want* me to dream.

My head is angry and thumps like a punch.

My throat and mouth are raw and gluey.

My stomach feels lonely and hollow and sour.

And my left foot hurts.

I sit up, my arms wrapped around my aching legs, my chin resting on my knees. I look out over the red, flat land before me. A heat-haze horizon blurring the sand and scrub up into the sky.

Then I twist my head and look behind me.

The same.

A vast expanse of nothingness. No buildings. No cars. No trucks. No bridges. No electricity pylons. No power stations. No railway tracks. No roads. No people. No lost shoe.

Nothing.

Just emptiness.

Everywhere.

The wind begins to blow dust off the ground and I hug my legs closer and shut my eyes.

Through the pounding of my head I try and think as hard as I can.

Think, think, think. I need to think.

There are three questions...

Three questions in my mind that I want to know the answers to right now.

The first question is – obviously – *Where am I?*

I feel as if this place is not the place to which I belong. It is too hot and too empty to be somewhere I belong. The one shoe on my foot does not look right for a place like this. The black dress I am wearing feels too soft for a place like this. Which leads my mind to the second question...

What am I doing here?

There must be some reason for me to be here. Some reason why I have found myself walking around – one shoe lost – in the middle of...well...nowhere. Everything happens for a reason, doesn't it? Don't people say that? I'm sure I have heard it before.

But it is the third question that worries me the most.

Or at least it is my inability to answer the third question that worries me.

I close my eyes even tighter and try to block out the landscape. I try to block out my headache. I block out my hunger and my thirst and I try to concentrate.

Okay, I think.

So...

Who am I?

PART ONE

Fugue – 1 A musical composition in which a short melody or phrase is introduced by one part and successively taken up by others.

2 A period during which someone loses their memory or sense of identity and may leave their home or usual surroundings.
(*Oxford English Dictionary*)

CHAPTER ONE
THE END

I've no idea how long I have been walking. Or where I've come from. Or where I'm going. Seconds, minutes, hours – they mean nothing to me.

I stumble on along what feels like the same strip of landscape, over and over and over and over again. Red dust desert with patches of small, wiry green bushes, endlessly reaching out in front of me.

The sun burns down from directly above – *does that mean it is midday?* – and the top of my head feels sore. So do my arms.

Looking behind, I see a trail. No footprints. My legs are too tired to actually lift my feet off the ground. Instead, I half drag them along, leaving a continuously twisting path that disappears between all the bushes somewhere back in the distance.

I keep moving and, after what feels like a very long time, I come to a small slanting rock jutting out of the dirt. It has a flat slice missing, just wide enough to sit on. I lean back against it, the heat in the rock burning my bottom and the tops of my legs through my dress. I rest the thing I carry on my lap.

This thing is a silvery, metallic box about a metre long with a handle in the middle. On either side of the handle are two locks. Each of the locks has three numbers that you have to turn. Line up the correct numbers and the locks will spring open. Only I don't know the numbers. Or, at least, I don't *remember* the numbers. Like I don't remember anything else.

I pick up a small rock from the ground and start banging at one of the locks. There might be something useful inside. Some food perhaps. Or something to drink. Something to help me survive in this weird wilderness. I slam and I slam but the rock doesn't help. It just buckles part of the lock slightly. I try the other one, slamming the rock down hard, hoping the lock will flick open.

It doesn't.

Dropping the rock back onto the earth, I clutch the box to my chest and shut my eyes.

Listen, I tell myself.

I try to listen.

If there is a road nearby, I might hear a car. Or if there is a railway track, I might hear a train.

So I listen.

But no. There is nothing. Just the sound of the wind blowing over the shrubs and around the rock, and the occasional squawk of a far-off bird.

That's all.

HELLO, I scream into red dust.

It doesn't answer.

WHERE AM I?

Hysterical.

Who's laughing?

I turn around.

Me.

A pool.

I see a pool.

Water!

I drag my body – heavy, now, so heavy – towards it. I am so tired. So thirsty.

But the pool moves away. It shimmers in the heat and clings to the horizon. I hold out one hand to tell it to stop. To stay where it is. But it keeps moving away.

I don't understand.

I don't understand.

I think time passes...

Air getting cooler. Sun drooping.

Pull the short sleeves of my dress down but they don't stretch further than my elbows.

A small pocket on the side of my dress...inside a green swirled marble. A *marble? Why am I carrying a marble?* Hold it up to the last glow of light and turn it around with dirt-cracked fingers, before slipping it back into the pocket.

I look around. Lost. Cold.

Please don't leave me out here in the dark, I say into the emptiness.

But only my heart answers.

I think the time has passed again.

Night smothers me.

Sounds...a flap of leathery wings, chit-chattering creatures, distant howls, snufflings close by.

Squeeze my ears and eyes tight after one peep at the cold frieze of stars and violent moonlight.

Breathing in and out, heart beating still...dozing in

and out of dreams. I am gliding…soaring…screaming…falling…

Then…

…the sun explodes, forcing my eyes wide to the same picture.

Endless red dust before and after.

Whimpering, sobbing.

Is that my voice? Is that me?

Don't leave me out here to die.

Somebody…save me…

Save—

Chapter Two

THE GIRL

"Hey!"

The voice wakes me like an electric shock.

"Hey!!"

I strain to lift my head from the ground. It is bright daytime and I can feel that the sun is angry again.

It is hard to open my eyes. The lids seem to have grown together – or at least that's how it feels, and it takes me a long time.

Eventually, I make out a girl. Standing above.

A slingshot outstretched and pointed straight at me.

A hard, round, silver ball bearing catching the morning sun and menacingly aimed at my head.

"What are you doing!?" I shout, panic suddenly flooding my veins.

I bring my hands up in front of my face. "What are

you doing?" I call again. "Don't shoot me!"

"Don't move!" the girl orders. "Don't…move."

She nods her head to indicate that there is something right behind me.

"Don't look!" she says through her teeth.

"How…am I…not meant to look when…you tell me… not to look?" I mutter, frightened, half aware that I am not making sense.

Somehow – perhaps it is just weakness – I manage not to look.

It feels like for ever that we are in that position. The girl with a taut slingshot, one eye shut to aim. Me lying oddly forward on the ground, my mouth open wide in fear.

"Right," says the girl quietly, like she is trying not to let whatever it is hear her words. "On the count of three, I'm going to shoot at it."

"What—?"

"Sssh!" she hisses. "On the count of three. Once I've shot…straight away, jump towards me. Roll forward. Whatever. On the ground. Okay? Before it strikes."

"Before it—"

"*Ssssssh!*"

I nod.

"Okay…one," the girl starts counting, "two…THREE!"

I hear the ball bearing *thwhistle* past my ear, and somehow I find the energy to quickly roll myself forward onto the ground before the girl's feet. Without stopping, I push myself over and straighten up, desperate to see whatever it was.

Beside me, the girl loads another shot into the sling and takes aim.

On the ground, about a metre from where I was just sitting, a long, rainbow-coloured snake – *iridescent is the word* – is retreating, whipping its body left and right, zig-zagging across the red sand to escape the shiny bolts the girl is unleashing against it.

Thwad. Another ball bearing buries itself in the dirt right next to the snake's head. It moves away even quicker.

"Gwardar," says the girl, catching the tip of its tail with another one. "Probably been right behind you all night. Trying to keep warm. When I saw it, it was getting closer to you – closer and closer. Think it was preparing to attack."

The snake keeps moving, churning the sand up with its twisting body.

"You think it was going to…bite me?" I ask, my right hand clutching the front of my dress.

"Oh, yeah," says the girl as if it was nothing. "Definitely."

Suddenly blackness overcomes me and I feel myself falling.

There is water on my lips.

I do not question it. I let it slide over my tongue and down to the back of my throat.

A hand on the back of my head and the hard plastic of a bottle rim on my lips. I drink the water up – some of it runs down the side of my cheek. Wasted.

"There," says a voice. "There."

I drink.

I swallow fast, desperate to ease the burning in my throat.

"Hey," says the voice. "Take it easy."

It is a female voice.

The girl's voice…

The bottle is removed from my lips. I try calling out for it to be returned, but then a hand – wet with water – runs over my brow, cooling my forehead. It feels so good.

"Wait here," the voice says. "I will be back soon. A few minutes. Don't move."

I hear feet scrunching against the dirt. Running. Away from me.

I raise my arms in the air. *Please don't go,* I try saying, but nothing comes out of my mouth. *Please stay. Don't leave me alone here.*

I wipe the dryness out of my eyes with the backs of my wrists and then push myself up into a sitting position. Slowly adjusting to the burning bright sun yet again, I look around.

There is nobody here.

But on the ground not five metres away from me is a cage.

At least it looks like a cage. But it is made of wood or bamboo or something. Sticks all curving over themselves until they knot together at the top.

I squint to see more clearly.

Surely it isn't a cage? It can't be a cage.

Then something moves inside.

The snake! I panic, remembering.

But no...

There is a flutter.

A bird?

It *is* a cage.

Next to the cage lies a full large canvas bag, its thick strap twisted over on top of itself. Jutting just out of the bag I can see a bottle of water.

I bend my legs and try to lift myself up, but they are

far too weak and I topple back onto the ground. I try again, but my legs just quiver underneath me and give way.

So, I crawl. Somehow I get up onto my knees and I crawl towards the bag. Centimetre by centimetre. My knees painful against the stones. When I get to the bag, I pull out the bottle, unscrew the top and start taking huge gulps of the water.

It tastes so good. I sit myself down next to the cage and drink.

"Hey!" I hear the voice behind me. "Don't drink it all. That's got to last another ten kilometres."

I twist my neck and look closely at the girl.

She is probably about thirteen years old. Her skin is brown, her long black hair pulled back in metal clips. She is wearing dirty denim dungarees and a pink stripy T-shirt under them. In her hands she carries what looks like an old handkerchief, filled with something. On her feet, cork sandals. In her pierced ears, miniature green and sparkling crocodiles.

She comes alongside me, puts the handkerchief on the ground and takes the water bottle from my hands.

"You can't just go and drink as much as you want, you know. Not out here." She puts the top on the bottle and slides it back into her bag. Then she pulls out a small knife. "You have to keep it rationed."

Her voice is high and sweet, but she doesn't speak too clearly.

The girl unravels the handkerchief. In the centre of it sit a number of small, greenish fruits. She takes one and cuts it with the knife.

"Billygoat plum," she says. The knife splits the fruit in half and she flicks a hard stone out of its centre. "Here." She holds one of the halves up to me. "Eat. It's really, really good for you. Loads of vitamins."

I take it and put it into my dry mouth. The fruit tastes good – like stewed apples. I chew on it – its juices soaking my tongue – then swallow. With difficulty. The girl hands me the other half.

"When I first saw you there, I thought you were dead," she says, splitting some more of the billygoat plums open. "I thought that you were already a goner. Thought you were a dingo's lunch. A gwardar's tasty treat."

I don't answer. I concentrate on chewing and swallowing.

The girl pulls a small wooden bowl out of her bag, followed by a perfectly round stone. She drops a couple of the plum halves into the bowl.

"I wasn't expecting to come across a dead body. Not today. Not any day, in fact." She picks up the stone and starts rolling it around the bowl, squashing the fruit inside. "So, it was a bit of a shock. Then I saw you moving."

She holds out the bowl to me.

"I saw you breathing. Then I saw the snake… Here," she says. "Rub this on your arms. They look real burnt to me."

I take the bowl and dip my fingers in the juice. Then I put some of it on my arm. It hurts.

"That's it. Rub it on. It will cool you down. It's not the best plant for that. There are others that do it better. But they don't grow around here."

I start to rub. Gently. Soon the billygoat juice soothes the pain, so I apply some to my other arm. And my face.

"Where's your shoe?" the girl asks, pointing to my filthy left foot.

I shrug.

She drags herself down to the bottom of my leg and lifts it slightly so she can see.

"Oooh. That's real nasty." She pulls a couple of thorns or stones out from the skin and moves her face nearer to get a better look. "Need to clean it up. Might go real bad if you don't. Might go green and smelly and drop off."

I look at her and she looks back at me.

"Only kidding. I'll get a whole load more billygoat plums. There's a big bush. In a ditch. Just over there.

We'll wash your foot in the juice. Then I'll make you a new shoe. Won't be as pretty as your other one, but it will keep the splinters out of your toes."

The girl moves me.

She bends down next to me, puts her head under my arm and lifts me up – we are about the same height. I push hard with my legs and do my best to keep my balance. Somehow we manage to stay upright.

It is only a few hundred metres to the ditch with the billygoat plum tree, but it feels like a million. The girl helps me limp across the desert and, when we get to the ditch, she moves in front of me and lets me rest against her back as she walks me down.

The tree is long and spindly, but so incredibly green with fruit. It is the greenest thing I have seen out here – in fact, it might well be the greenest thing I have ever seen. The leaves shake in the slight breeze and – this is the best thing – they make a wide patch of shade on the ground. A huge circular patch that covers one side of the ditch.

The girl practically carries me to the shade before dropping me down on the ground. Then she runs back to collect her bag and the cage before returning.

"How long has it been since you've eaten anything?" she asks. "Not counting the plums I just gave you."

I shake my head.

She pulls a whole load more plums down.

"These are for your foot. I don't think you'd better eat many more. Not yet anyway. Your belly won't be able to handle it. It's been real empty so you'll get a bad bellyache. These plums are only just ripe too."

I lie back in the shade, my eyes closed as the girl uses the juice from the plums to clean out the sores and blisters on my foot. After a few soothing minutes she lowers it back to the ground.

"There you are. As good as a new thing. Well, almost."

She shuffles alongside me before cutting another of the billygoat plums and popping each half into her mouth.

"So how long have you been out in the bush?" she asks, her dark eyes staring down at me.

I make a face.

"Do you speak?" she says. "Or has the bunyip got your tongue?"

I sit up and cross my legs. I cough to clear the last of the dryness from my throat.

"I don't know," I say.

"You don't know if you can speak or you don't know how long you've been in the bush?"

"I don't know how long I've been out here," I say.

"Yeah, well, that makes sense."

"I don't even know where I am," I add. "I mean, I don't even know *where in the world* I am."

"Whoa!" barks the girl. "You really *are* lost."

I nod. "Yes. I am."

The girl pulls her water bottle from out of her canvas bag, removes the top and hands it to me.

"Australia," she says as I take a couple of small sips. "You're right in the middle of Australia. Northern Territory. Does that help?"

Chapter Three

THE BELLBIRD

As the afternoon moves on, I try to rest in the shade of the tree. I slip in and out of sleep, exhausted by everything, and dream of things I do not remember. Whenever I wake up, all the dreams fade away, and I am still as lost as ever.

And that frightens me so much.

The girl sits on the edge of the ditch and watches. At one point I wake to see her stitching together some rough strips of fabric. She twists a thick needle in and out of the strips – a dark, coarse-looking thread trailing behind it. Then she comes down and holds the thing she is making up against my bare foot before going back and readjusting it.

"That dress you're wearing," she says when she sees I am awake again. "That's not exactly ideal bush wear.

35

And your shoes…I mean your *shoe*. Not really designed for this kinda land." She flips the fabric over and starts stitching again. "I'd've thought a city girl like you should be wearing a good solid pair of walking boots."

I lift my head to look at her. "City girl?"

"Sure," she says. "I can tell. The cut of your hair. Your smooth hands. The expensive shoe. Where're you from? Brisbane? Perth?"

I reach up and feel my hair, lifting it so I can see. It is long and blonde and feels as if – once upon a time, long, long ago – it was soft and well brushed. However, now it is clumped and knotted and full of leaves.

"You must know something," the girl continues, her eyes concentrating on her needlework. "Everyone knows something. Everyone knows their name."

I prop myself on my elbows. "I don't."

She puts the fabric on the ground in front of her. "You can't even remember your own name? Jeez. That's rough. So…what're you saying? You just woke up one morning and found yourself out here? Hundreds of kilometres from anywhere?"

Hundreds of kilometres from anywhere? That frightens me even more.

"And you've no idea why you're here?" She points to the box. "So, what's in that?"

I turn to look at it and shrug.

"You think it might be a gun? I've seen guns in cases like that." She gets up, wipes the dust on her hands on the sides of her dungarees and picks up the box by its handle. She lifts it to her ear and gives it a shake. "Perhaps you're a hunter, out stalking a rogue croc. If you are, you're the best dressed croc hunter I've ever seen." She drops the case to the floor and starts playing with its locks. "What's the code to open it? Oh… Silly question…"

"I tried smashing the locks," I explain. "With a rock. But I couldn't open it."

The girl pulls a second, even longer and wider knife out from her canvas bag. "Let me try." She pushes the knife under one of the locks and tries levering it up, leaning her weight on the handle. I see the muscles tensing in her arm as she forces the knife down as far as she can. After a minute, she gives up and tries to do the same thing on the other lock.

"No!" she almost shouts. "Whatever's in this box doesn't wanna come out. Must be something important, though."

I watch as she rubs her fingers around the cold, steely sides and the metal bolts that run all the way along the edges. "No. This is one tough case, that's for sure. Tough and expensive."

"Is it?" I say, not really knowing what to say. "I wouldn't know."

The girl laughs. "Well there's not much you *do* know at the moment, is there?"

I try to smile.

"There's one thing you *should* know, I suppose," she says, taking up her sewing again, "and that's my name." She leans over and offers me her hand to shake. "I'm Tarni. Werte!"

"Shouldn't we be moving on?" I ask as the afternoon sun slowly moves around us. "I mean, it's getting late now, so if we are going to get anywhere before the sun goes down, I think we'd better—"

"We're not going anywhere tonight," says Tarni, feeding little bits of…something…to the thing in the cage.

"Why?" I suddenly feel as if I am going to panic. Blood seems to be gushing through my head and my heart, and my chest feels tight. "I mean…I mean…we can't just stay out here overnight. I did that LAST NIGHT and I don't think I want to do it AGAIN. It gets so dark. And there are animals…" My eyes scan the ground around us. "Snakes and things."

"I'm afraid it's quite a way to the next waterhole," says Tarni like it doesn't mean anything. "Almost a day's walking – and I don't think you're fit enough to do it today. You're weak and you need to rest. You need to get some real good sleep tonight. We'll set out in the morning. Soon after first light."

"But…but isn't there a town or a farm or something nearby?" I hear the desperation in my voice. "There must be something! Nowhere can be as deserted as all that. Surely there's somewhere we can go to for help? Don't you have a mobile? Can't you call somebody?"

Tarni laughs and drops what looks like another dried worm into the cage.

"No. No mobile. And no town. Not out here. We're a long way from anywhere. But if you come with me, I'll keep you safe." She pushes her fingers between the bars of the cage. "But…you'll need to keep up with me tomorrow. I don't want you slowing me down. You slow me down and I'll leave you behind, right? Then you'll have to make your own way across the outback – and from what I've seen of you so far, I don't fancy your chances."

Then something strange happens.

Like a flash in my head.

A memory? Of voices.

Come on. We need to hurry up, says someone. *We're going to be late. Why are you always so slow?*

I don't know whose voice it is. I don't know if it is male or female. I can't tell if it's old or young. It's like an echo in my mind.

But then I hear another voice. My own voice. I hear myself laughing.

Why do you worry about other people so much? I ask bitterly. *If we're late, then we're late. It's tough. No problem. Let them all wait.*

And, a billionth of a second later, as suddenly as it arrived, the memory – if that's what it was – is gone.

I shake my head and stare at the girl.

"So, whatever you do, don't slow me down," she finishes.

I suddenly feel irritated by her, but I clamp it all inside as my brain tries to clutch hopelessly for the memory again.

"Oh, and you need to have a name," she says. "I can't avoid saying your name just because you don't know what it is. I can't just call you 'hey' or 'girl' or something like that. You need to have a name."

"But—"

"I know!" Tarni clicks the fingers of her hand not poking into the cage. "I got it! Moonflower. That's what I'll call you."

"Moonflower?"

"Yeah."

"Isn't that a bit of a...*weird* name?" I ask sarcastically.

"So what?"

"Well..."

"A moonflower is a very pretty thing," says Tarni. "Its flowers come out at night and hide away in the daytime. Some types only bloom once a year. That makes them real special."

"Ha! I don't think anybody's called Moonflower," I say. "It's not a *proper* name, is it? And I *definitely* don't think my real name's anything like that at all. I have a feeling my actual name's something much nicer."

"Well, that's perfect then." Tarni grins. "Until your *real* nice name suddenly comes back into your head, you can have a *real* deadly one."

I think I must look confused. "Deadly?"

"Yeah. Deadly. Amazing. Excellent. *Deadly*."

"Oh."

Suddenly, a loud noise seems to attack my ears. It is high pitched and like a bell being rattled over and over again, very *very* fast. I put my hands over my ears to block the noise and Tarni laughs out loud.

The noise, I realize, is coming from the cage.

When it stops almost as suddenly, I lower my hands.

"What was that?" I say. "*What* is in that cage?"

"Have you never heard the call of a bellbird before?" she asks.

Tarni shakes her head and moves the cage so it is sitting between us. "*This* is a bellbird. I found him a couple of days back. You don't normally see them around here. This area is far too dry. They usually prefer the coast or forests so he must have been blown inland somehow. Poor thing. One of his wings was broken and he was just limping along the ground. If I'd left him alone, a dingo or a snake would have killed and eaten him within hours, so I built this cage. I'm feeding him up until his wing is fixed. Then I'm going to set him free."

I lean down and look between the bent wooden bars. Inside I see a drab, green little bird with a dull orange beak and dirty orange feet. He is perched on a stick that Tarni has wedged across the middle of the cage.

"It makes a lot of noise for such a small, weird-looking bird," I say. "Does it do that often?"

"Quite a lot," says the girl with a sort of despairing look on her face. "I've named him Candelabra by the way."

I think I must raise my eyebrows.

"Yeah, I know," says Tarni with pride. "Another deadly name."

42

The ground is hard and stony and difficult to rest on. I move myself around in an attempt to get comfortable again, but I can't. It's impossible. So, I just lie there as much as I can with my eyes closed, huffing slightly to myself as I listen to Tarni making a fire. After a while, I smell smoke and hear a loud crackling, so I prop myself up on my elbows again.

"You know you snore," says Tarni, poking the glowing, flickering fire with a thick stick.

"I do *not* snore," I splutter back at her.

"You do. You snore louder than a yowie in the Dreamtime. When you were asleep earlier you were making the branches of that tree rattle." She points up to the tree behind me.

"Rubbish! I don't snore. You must have imagined it."

Tarni twitches her nose then goes back to poking at the food cooking on the fire.

"I don't snore," I mutter under my breath, but I don't even know my name so how can I be so definite? "Anyway," I ask as a way of distracting myself from my own uncertainty, "what's a…yowie?"

"A yowie?" She prods the fire some more. "This land is full of spirits that walk across it. Spirits of ancestors that take care of the land and protect it and its people.

But a yowie is a spirit *monster* – not all spirits are good, y'know? It looks like a human but it's covered in hair or fur, all over its body. It's taller than any man and has the strength of three gorillas. Some people say it comes into your house or your hut at night and steals you. Takes you into the woods and rips your arms and legs off and eats you. Leaves your bones in a nice neat pile."

She smiles at me.

"My uncle says he saw one once." She waves the stick in the air. "Around here. Says he was off tracing a dreaming track when a yowie came running at him, its arms above its head like it was going to smash him to death. Says it was making the most horrible noise he'd ever heard."

"What did your uncle do?" I shift forward to hear.

"He did the best thing he could do. He ran away. Real, real fast. He dropped all his stuff and took off. Didn't stop to look behind him. Just turned his feet into dust."

I look up and see that the sky is darkening quickly.

"He saw one…around…here?" I ask.

"So he said," says Tarni. "But he *does* make his own booze in a barrel. And he drinks most of it himself. So I wouldn't completely trust him."

Tarni turns back to the fire. The air is getting cold again and the warmth from the fire feels welcome.

"I'm cooking us some dinner," says Tarni. "You've probably had enough of the billygoat plums."

I look at the fire again. On one side I can see a tiny saucepan sitting at a tricky angle on top of some glowing embers. Steam seems to be smoking out of the top.

On the opposite side of the fire to me I see that Tarni has got something skewered with a metal spike, both ends resting on top of some rocks. Again, it is slightly out of the direct flames, cooking over some red-hot ash.

I look at Tarni and she grins.

"In the pot I've got some parkily. It's a vegetable. A herb. You can find it out here – if you know where to look, that is." She looks quite proud of herself. "It's usually hidden away in all the aywerte – the little green bushes that you see everywhere."

"The spiky ones?"

"That's right. The ones you can't escape. The ones that are everywhere. They are aywerte." Tarni points to the ground next to the fire. "Under there, I've put a couple of bush potatoes. Anatye. You put them in the ground next to the fire and they cook. Slowly. They don't taste too deadly, but they'll fill up your belly. And if you mix the parkily with it, you can pretend that it's not something completely irntirte."

"And what's that?" I ask. "On the skewer?"

"Oh, a rabbit."

"You found a rabbit? Out here?"

She looks proud of herself again.

"And you killed it?" I ask.

Her face is suddenly confused. "Of course I killed it. How else are we meant to eat it?"

"But rabbits… You can't kill rabbits…they're cute."

Tarni shakes her head. "Rabbits ain't cute. Rabbits are a pest. There're millions of them all over the bush. They eat all the plants that keep the desert in place and then the desert starts to move."

"I don't know what you mean."

Tarni sighs. "I don't understand you. You can't even remember your own name and where you come from, but you *can* remember that a rabbit looks cute."

"How did you catch the rabbit?" I say, distracting myself again from these worrying thoughts. "Did you use a snare?"

Tarni shakes her head. "No. Snares are nasty." She taps the side of her nose with her finger. "Used an old Alyawarre trick. Always works. The bunny wouldn't have felt a thing." She continues tapping her nose. "Secret."

After what feels like a very long time, Tarni announces that supper is ready.

"I only have one bowl," she says. "So, you'll have to eat out of the pan. Once it's cool enough."

Tarni drains the dribble of water out of the leaves cooking in the pan and sets them aside. Then she uses a stick to prise the bush potatoes out of the hot earth. She pushes them onto a small mat, then starts peeling their skins – steam billowing out as she does so. Using a small knife, she slices the potatoes up.

Then she turns her attention to the rabbit.

Pulling the skewer out of the rabbit, she places it on the mat next to the cooling potatoes. Then she slices the meat off the bones, using her fingers to pull off any small and awkward parts.

The whole thing looks disgusting to me and I find myself having to look away.

"There you are, Moonflower!"

I turn back. Tarni holds out the pan to me, a strange wooden spoon sticking out of the top. In her other hand is the wooden bowl that she used to break up the billygoat plums earlier today.

Suddenly, like before, there is a flash in my head.

Another memory?

I am staring down at a plate with swirls along the edge.

In the middle of the plate sits a blobby pile of green and orange and slightly yellow stuff. I feel myself twirling a shiny fork in my fingers.

You must *eat it*, says the voice that I still can't nail down. *It's very good for you. Kale and lentil salad.*

Mmmm. Delicious. I hear my voice, sarcastic again. *I can't wait. Looks wonderful.*

The other voice tries to ignore me. *It's full of vitamins. Full of minerals. Cleansing. Precisely the sort of thing successful people eat.*

Oh lucky them, I hear myself saying. *Perhaps they can have my helping too. Perhaps I can put it in an envelope and post it to them.*

And then...

Gone.

What is going on?

"Here." Tarni is thrusting the steaming pan towards me. "Take it."

I look down at it disdainfully.

"Can't *you* eat out of the pan?" I ask. "I mean...I don't think it's the kind of thing *I* normally do. Eat out of... a pan."

Tarni's face falls into a frown.

"Are you the queen of Australia?"

"What?"

"I don't believe I've ever met a real queen before." She bows her head. "Pleased to meet you, Your Majesty. How honoured I am to have you here eating with me in my humble camp." She lifts her head and pushes the pan towards me. "No." Her voice changes. "The pan's yours."

Reluctantly, I take it from her. The handle is hot and I have to put it on the ground in front of me. The scent drifts up towards my nose.

It really does smell delicious.

Chapter Four

THE HOLE

Later in the evening, Tarni takes a thin colourful blanket out of her big canvas bag and lays it across me.

"You have the rug tonight," she says. "I'll kip next to the fire. I always prefer kipping next to a fire. It feels more natural. Anyway, it means I can keep an eye on it and feed it with sticks whenever it gets low."

This makes me nervous. "Won't a fire attract wildlife?"

"Wildlife? Nah. Fires tend to keep wildlife away. Scares it all off. Also, any animal that usually comes out at night…well, they are designed to see in the dark. The fire is too bright for them. It hurts their eyes."

I feel relieved. Well, slightly.

"The only animal to worry about at night near a fire is a snake. They like to warm themselves up next to one."

"Oh. Yes. I remember."

I pull the blanket over me and make a point of tucking it tightly under my sides.

During the night, I dream.

I don't know what it is I am dreaming of exactly, but I know that it is something I know well.

A pattern. Repeated over and over again. In little squares.

A diamond within a diamond within a diamond.

The first diamond is a light blue colour – or, at the very least, it *feels* light blue.

The second diamond looks (or feels) a deep burgundy colour.

The third and smallest diamond, a rich green.

All inside a square.

And to the left and to the right and above and below it, exactly the same pattern. And to the left and to the right and above and below those, the exact same pattern.

Over and over and over and over.

Again and again and again.

As far as I can see.

The sound of an alarm clock.

A loud, high-pitched ringing that rattles around inside my skull and seems to shake my brain awake. I open my eyes expecting to reach out and push the *off* button on the clock, only to find myself staring into the bright light of the early morning sun and the image of a girl poking her finger through the bars of a wooden cage.

"Shut it, you crazy kwepalpale," says Tarni to the screeching bellbird. "I think we've kinda got the message. Here –" she picks something up from the ground – "have a stink bug for breakfast." She pushes it into the cage and the bellbird stops its terrible ringing noise. "Good morning, Moonflower."

I sit up and throw the rug off my aching legs. I feel dirty and sweaty already – *when was the last time I washed? When was the last time I felt clean? Whenever it was, it was* far *too long ago* – and I pull a couple of sticks out of my hair before dropping them onto the smouldering patch of ash where the fire has now died.

"Here!" Tarni throws me something. I catch it. "Try it on. It will fit."

It is the strange shoe thing she was sewing together for me last night. It looks more like a sock than a shoe, only with a thicker, more leathery sole.

I pull it on over my foot.

It fits perfectly.

I stand up and take a few steps, trying it out.

"How is it?"

I can't feel the stones on the ground and, suddenly, I think that I might actually be able to walk without the sores on my feet reopening.

I nod.

"Like I said, it's not pretty, but it will do the job." Tarni takes up the rug and folds it neatly back into her canvas bag. "Now, I suppose you want breakfast?"

"Of course."

"Here!" She throws something else at me. It is a lump of something very dry and very hard.

"What's this?"

"Wattleseed bread. An old woman in my community bakes it. Gave me a monster big loaf before I set off."

I sniff it. "It's stale."

"No. It's like that from the time it comes out of the oven. It's okay. You can eat it. It's not poisoned."

I take a bite. It is chewy. Nutty. Not very nice.

"It's better with something spread on it, but out here it's hard to find a tub of peanut butter or jelly." Tarni pulls the water bottle out of her bag and hands it to me. "I have two bottles that I always take with me. This is the second."

I look at the bottle and see that it is about two-thirds full.

"Six mouthfuls. That's all you can have this morning. We'll stop later on and have more. But we have to keep it rationed. When we get to the next waterhole, we'll fill them both up."

I finish off the wattleseed bread, take off the top and put the bottle to my lips. I try to make my six mouthfuls as big as possible.

"Don't gulp," says Tarni. "I can see you're gulping."

I reluctantly hand her the bottle and she puts it back into her bag.

"Okay, Moonflower," she says, pulling the bag off the ground and swinging it over and onto her shoulder. "Let's get moving." She picks up the bellbird in the cage and starts to walk off.

"Wait," I call. She stops and turns round to look at me. "Are we going *right now*? Was that all we had for breakfast? Some bread and some water?" My stomach makes a noise as if it is agreeing with me. "I mean, it wasn't very much, was it? Surely there's something else we can eat?"

Tarni sighs, then puts a hand into a pocket on the front of her denim dungarees. She pulls something out and tosses it towards me.

I catch it.

It is a billygoat plum.

"There," she says. "Eat it as we walk."

Tarni is not slow.

She is strong and fast and leaves me behind.

"Keep up," she shouts back to me. "You need to be quicker." She turns away and marches on, no change in her step.

I try. I follow her but my feet are sore and my legs are tired and my head is throbbing and my mouth is dry.

And the flies are driving me insane.

There are millions of them. Everywhere. But mostly around my head. They buzz into my ears and across my eyes. They land on my arms and face. Then, after I've brushed them off, they land again. I wave my hand in front of me, hoping to scare them away. But they aren't scared.

In the end I start to speed up, trying to outrun them.

Tarni sees me.

"That's it," she shouts. "That's better. Keep going *that* speed."

An hour or two later and my legs are in agony. Two different types of shoe don't help, but Tarni always keeps herself twenty, thirty, forty metres ahead of me. All I can do is follow. And Tarni doesn't falter. She walks on with as much energy as the first step she took this morning.

So, when I see her climb on top of a bulky looking rock, sit down and start pulling out the loaf of wattleseed bread, my soul breathes a sigh.

My body is too exhausted to be able to scramble up the rock, so Tarni leans over, holds out her hand and helps pull me up. I have to leave my long metal case down on the ground so that I can use my other hand to steady me.

The rock feels hot under this relentless sun. Tarni pulls her rug out and stretches it across the stone. Then we sit on it. She passes me a chunk of the bread.

"My people call this Lookout Rock."

"Is that because you can see a long way from here?" I stare into the distance. Everywhere everything still looks exactly the same. Flat, red and dry.

"Nah," Tarni replies. "It's because one of my ancestors fell off it once. 'Look out!' the people shouted at him, but he didn't hear them."

"Oh," I say.

We eat the bread. It is absolutely awful but I suppose

at least it is helping the squelches in my stomach to lessen.

"I had a thought," says Tarni eventually. "Just now. I don't reckon you've managed to remember much about yourself yet?"

I think about the two tiny slivers of memory that never really formed, and I shake my head.

"So…" She puts her hand deep into her bag and pulls out a little flat rectangle. "Have a look at this."

I take it from her and twist it over.

It is a very cloudy and slightly cracked mirror.

"Go on." She nods. "Look at your face. See if that helps you remember who you are."

I hold it up in front of me.

In the mirror, staring back at me, is a girl with bright blue eyes. They look tired. Her nose is small and neat, her lips thin and dry. Her white hair is long and straggly and looks as if it could do with a good wash. With shampoo. Her face is dirty, with a wide oily smear down one cheek. And on the other cheek is a scar. A short but very red-looking cut. It looks fresh.

The girl looks about thirteen years old.

I do not recognize her.

I reach up and touch the scar on the strange girl's cheek. It stings a little. *How did I get this?*

"Anything?" asks Tarni. "Do you know who you are now?"

"No," I say, still looking at myself in the imperfect mirror. "I don't."

I want to know this girl staring back at me. I really do. I want to say, Ah yes, that's…whoever. I'm whoever. *But I can't. I am still as impossible to know as this land. And I don't understand why. Why don't I know who I am? Why don't I recognize myself in the mirror?*

All these thoughts crashing through my head are making me feel even more confused. And lost. And angry. So I throw down the mirror.

"Hey!" says Tarni, leaning forward to catch it before it slips off the end of the rock. "Don't do that. It's cracked enough. Break it any more and you'll get seven years of bad luck."

"I don't care!" I snap. "I don't care if I get seven years of bad luck…or if *you* get seven years of bad luck. None of it matters if I don't know who I am." In my mind – my rational mind – I think that I am being a bit *too* grouchy but, for some reason, I just can't seem to stop myself. It's almost like I'm designed to be this angry.

"Still…there's no need to slam down the mirror like that," she says, putting it back into her bag. "I was just trying to help."

I shake my head. "But I don't know who I am. I don't even know who *you* are. I mean… Tell me, Tarni…I don't understand. What are you doing here? Why are you out here…?" I sweep my arm to show the vast emptiness around us. "All alone. It doesn't make any sense to me."

Tarni wipes the wattleseed crumbs deliberately from her lips like she hasn't heard me.

"Tarni!" I almost shout. "Why aren't you at home with your family? I mean, where are they? Where is your home?"

She raises her eyebrows. "My home? Utopia. It's a small Alyawarre town," she explains. "Not much there. Just a few humpies. A store. A doctor's surgery. A few stripped-down trucks and cars." She shrugs. "Nothing much."

"Is that where we're going? Utopia? Is that where you're taking me?"

Tarni laughs and practically spits the last bits of wattleseed over the edge of the rock. "No. We're not."

"You're *not* leading me back to your home?" I can sense the panic in my voice again.

"Oh, no. Utopia's about fifty kilometres –" she points in the direction of where we've just come – "that way. We're not going back there. Not now."

"Then…where are…where are we headed?"

"Well…Utopia's *that* way…and I'm heading –" she puts her finger in the opposite direction – "*this* way."

I wait for a few seconds expecting her to say more. "Yes? And?"

"Hmm?"

"Well…" I sigh. "*Why* are we going *that way*? *What* is over there?"

"According to the song, in about five more k, there's water. Loads of it."

"Song?"

She doesn't hear me.

"And where there's water, there's food. There'll be fruit to collect and animals to catch. And not just rabbits. Birds. Tasty birds." Her brown eyes are wide and bright. "With luck, Moonflower, tonight we will have a real feast."

We push on across the dust, around the spiky aywerte and into the unbearable heat of the middle of the day. Even the breeze is hot out here and my black dress sticks like gum on an envelope.

There are blisters on my fingers from the handle of the case, and my arms are covered in a dull ache from its weight. I don't know why I persist in carrying it. I don't know why I don't just drop it to the ground and leave it where it falls, sparing my hands and arms the misery. But like the perfectly round, green-striped marble in my pocket, I hold on to it because I know what it stands for. It stands for the truth. About me. About who I am.

So I'm not going to let it go.

Not until I know the truth about myself.

With no other choice, my grip tightens.

I try singing to myself. I don't know what it is I am singing, but I seem to be pulling music from somewhere inside my confused mind. It isn't much – a short melody of something – but it cheers me up.

All the answers to all my questions must surely be somewhere inside my head, mustn't they? It is simply a matter of allowing them out...

I sing the tune louder and my legs seem to grow stronger. I see Tarni turning her head to look at me. She smiles and waves before marching on.

Soon the landscape changes. Slightly. It is still as red as Mars and as dusty as the moon, but there is a ridge directly in front of us. The ground moves upwards and it is not so flat. It is not a mountain. It is not even a hill. Just a small incline, rough and rocky.

Tarni waits for me at the bottom.

"You sounded real perky just now," she says. "People's brains get hot in the sun sometimes. They start imagining loads of things. Doing stuff they wouldn't normally do."

"I was just singing!" I mutter. Then I remember something. "But…wait…the other day. Before you found me. I thought I saw a pool. I kept moving towards it…but I never got there."

"Mirage. It looks like water but it's not. Just the—" she wobbles her left hand in front of me. "Just the heat making the ground look all shaky. Making it look like there's a big lake or something right in front of your eyes. I see them all the time. You don't know if they're real or not. Anyway," she drops her hand to her side, "don't worry about that. Come on!" Tarni starts making her way up the ridge. She struggles to keep her balance with the canvas bag over her shoulder and the birdcage in her left hand.

I follow behind, struggling myself with the case.

It gets steeper towards the top. And the ground becomes more like shale, making each footstep harder to take than the last. I see Tarni standing on the peak, peering down to whatever is beyond.

Eventually, I manage it and I find myself standing next to Tarni.

On the other side of the ridge, the ground drops away again, sloping more gently to the usual flat, red landscape. The only difference being that, not too far away from the ridge...

I rub my eyes with the palms of my hands.

A pool.

A *pool?*

I point to it.

"Is *that* a mirage?" I ask Tarni. "Am I imagining *that?*"

"Nah." Tarni grins an enormous grin. "That one's real. See, I told you it was here."

The pool is long and wide, and the light from the sun and the soft hot breeze make glittering ripples across its surface. Flocks of birds are clustered around its edge and in the shallows.

"COOEE!"

I jump. Tarni has dropped the cage to the ground, cupped her hands round her mouth and made the most extraordinary noise.

"COOOOOOEEEEEE!"

The birds take off, like clouds. Up into the sky and over to a place of safety from where they watch.

Tarni looks at me.

"It's our turn now."

I can barely control myself as I scramble down the

other side of the ridge. I get ahead of Tarni and drop my case onto the earth before racing towards the pool. I feel so dirty and sticky and sweaty. All I want to do is throw myself into the water. I don't even bother to take my shoes off. I run into the water, the cool wetness splashing over my legs and soaking my dress. I turn round and fall backwards into it, feeling the heat suffocated by this beautiful lake.

I see Tarni waving at me.

She looks anxious.

She is calling.

I try to hear.

"…crocs!"

Crocs?

I jump out quicker than I fell in.

I rush out, looking over my shoulder at the water.

"There are crocodiles?" I ask.

Tarni comes alongside me. "Sometimes there *are* and sometimes there *ain't*. Crocs are crafty little fellas. They like to keep themselves under the surface. Watching everything going on. Waiting until something gets a bit too near. And then…SNAP! Dinner is served."

I suddenly feel very ill.

Tarni stares past me and surveys the pool. "Luckily for you, Moonflower…this hole's far too shallow."

I am sitting on Tarni's rug a few metres back from the edge of the watering hole – it feels like I'm sunbathing at the beach – and I watch as Tarni makes a fire.

Firstly, she pushes a circle of rocks in the dust, then finds a whole load of sticks and dried grasses, piling them up in the middle of the rock ring.

Next, Tarni pulls over her bag and takes out what looks like a rough, round stone and a long, rectangular strip of metal.

"Flint and steel," she explains. "This," she holds up the stone to me, "is the flint. And this," she holds up the metal strip, "is the steel. If I bash them together it makes sparks. You ever used a flint and steel before?"

I make a face as if to say *what do you think?*

Tarni starts to knock the two things together and sparks begin to jump out onto the ground. Eventually, one of the sparks lands on the nest of dried grass, and it begins to burn. Tarni blows on the nest until it bursts completely into flame. Then she slowly feeds sticks onto it.

"And that," says Tarni, "is how you make a fire."

Over the next hour, she shows me her elaborate method of purifying water. I vaguely take in that it involves boiling the pool water, letting it cool off, then straining it through what looks like an old sock, but I'm too busy thinking about myself to fully understand.

Instead, I try and ignite the dried grasses of the memories hidden away within me. Try and use the flint and steel of my mind to spark them back to life.

I think about the pattern dream. I think about the flashes of memory. I think about the metal case. I think about the marble in my pocket. I think about the dress I wear. I think about all the little things that might open up some clue as to who I am and what I'm doing here.

I think of them individually. Then I try pairing them up. *What have the marble and the case got in common? What is the link between the patterns that repeat over and over again and the silky black dress?*

Then I picture them all together. One on top of the other in a big pile. Looking for the spark that opens everything up.

But…

I see nothing.

I still know nothing.

So I punch the ground and suddenly feel like crying.

Tarni tidies her things back into the canvas bag before opening up the cage and reaching in for the bellbird.

She pulls Candelabra out, clutching him tight in her hands.

"Let's take a look at you, mister."

Candelabra is a strange-looking bird. Dirty green feathers, and dull orange feet and beak that make him seem a little like a sort of grubby, tired clown. He looks clumsy and squat, and I can't imagine him flying at all.

Tarni holds him up above her head. The bird twists and wriggles, its head and beak jerking from left to right.

"You're a beauty," says Tarni. "A real beauty." I smile to myself. *Beauty?* "Now…let's see this terrible wing of yours."

She pulls Candelabra close to her chest and, with one hand, prises out the bird's right wing.

"Okay, boy. No need to panic. There, there. Ssssh." Her voice sounds as soothing as the water. "It's all okay."

The bird's head stops jerking quite so comically. It is like he is being calmed by this creature holding onto him.

Tarni stretches out the wing and inspects it.

"Ho, little bird," she whispers. "It is all okay. You're fixing up real good." She flexes the wing in and out. In and out. "Oh, yeah. You'll be taking to the wind real soon. Flying back to the place you came from." Tarni turns to me. "Watch this," she says and sets the bird down on the ground between us.

Candelabra slightly fluffs up his feathers and twists his head to look at Tarni and then to me. He waddles a couple of steps, then stops.

Tarni picks something tiny – a bug, I think – off the ground and holds it in front of Candelabra's beak.

"Hey, Candelabra," Tarni whispers. "Do you like spaghetti?" Tarni moves the bug left and right and the bird shakes his head following it. "You don't? Okay. What about dirty burgers? Do you like them?" She moves the bug left and right again and Candelabra appears to emphatically say no. "No? You're real fussy, aren't you?"

I find myself snorting.

"*You* ask him," says Tarni.

"Me? No. It's just silly."

"Go on. Ask him something."

I sigh.

"Okay…erm…Candelabra…do you like…" I say the first thing that comes into my head, "…ice cream sundaes?"

Candelabra says no.

"Lamington cakes?"

No.

"All this talk of food is making me even hungrier, you know. How about bugs?" I ask. "Bet you like a really disgusting, squashy bug, don't you, you repulsive little bird?"

Tarni moves her hand up and down and Candelabra nods in approval.

"Finally! We've found something you like to eat!" says Tarni before feeding the bug to Candelabra and easing him back inside his cage.

"You made that cage for him?" I ask.

Tarni nods. "From some stuff I found around."

I nod back.

Tarni smiles and sits up straighter. With pride. "I like to make things. I like to find stuff and—"

It is then that I spot the white line scratching itself into the blue of the sky above.

"Hey!" I jump up. "Hey! Look at that!"

Tarni stops talking, covers her eyes and looks at where my finger is pointing.

"It's a plane!" I almost shout. "Up there! Can you see it? A plane! That's its vapour trail."

"Yes."

"Well, they could rescue us! If we make enough noise, wave our arms, they might see us! Come on!"

I leap about, my arms flapping wildly.

"HEY!" I shout. "DOWN HERE! HELP US!! WE ARE LOST!!"

69

I feel my bare feet burning on the hot earth.

"HEEEY!!! DOWN HERE! WHOOO-HOOOO! HELP US!"

Tarni still sits on the ground, watching me.

"DOWN HERE! PLEEEEASE!!! WE NEED HELP!"

The plane's vapour trail keeps on in a straight line.

"PLEEEEEEEEEEEEASE! WE NEED HELP!!"

"It is too far up," says Tarni.

"WHAT?" I still shout.

"The plane is too far up in the sky. It's a commercial airline. Probably going to Japan or the United States. Somewhere abroad. It won't see you from that height."

"But…" I stand still. "It must. It has to."

"No. It won't. It's too high up and there are clouds between us and them. Look. We're not even dots to them. Anyway," she continues, "what makes you think we're lost? What makes you think we need help?"

"Well…duh…" I sweep my arm across to show the landscape. "LOOK."

"Look at what?"

"THIS. All of THIS. All of this…desert."

Tarni shakes her head and closes her eyes. "Just because *you* do not know where you are does not mean that *I* do not know where I am. I know exactly where I'm going."

"Where are we then?" I ask with too much anger in my voice. "Where is this place?"

"The area is Anmatjere," she answers.

"And does *anybody* live in…"

"Anmatjere. Some people, yes. First Country people mostly. Like me."

"Then where are they? How is it I haven't seen ANYONE ELSE in…days?"

Tarni stands up and stretches her legs. She seems unfazed by my sudden outburst. "They are scattered all across. It is a wide and open area. For each person in this land, there are hundreds and hundreds of kilometres. Not like in cities where the people are packed together like bricks in a wall."

I look up at the plane. It is moving further and further away.

"What if we write the word HELP on the ground? Drag a stick over the earth or – even better – spell it out with big rocks and logs and things. Make it *really* big."

Tarni shakes her head. "They still won't be able to see it. Too far up."

"They *might*."

"They won't."

"But they *might*!"

Tarni looks sad for me, like I do not know what I am talking about.

"You need a hat to keep the sun off your head," she says. "I will make you one."

CHAPTER FIVE

THE OLD WOMAN

I watch as Tarni takes her big knife and starts stripping long, waxy leaves from a pandanus tree. She cuts away the spikes along the side of each leaf and then, with tough strands of grass, ties a couple of them together to make a circle.

Then she sits on the ground, legs crossed, and starts weaving more pandanus leaves in and out of the circle, and in and out of themselves. She doesn't say anything as she does it, her eyes concentrating on the job.

It is weirdly fascinating. I watch her hands pulling leaves through and pushing them out, twisting and tying grass and tucking stray ends away. It feels like a long time but, at the end of it, Tarni hands me a solid-looking hat, green with a wide brim that goes all the way round.

"It will weigh a lot to start off," she says. "It will feel

73

heavy on your head. But, over days, the leaves will dry out and it will get lighter."

I try it on. Like the stitched together shoe that she made me yesterday, the hat fits perfectly.

"You know…I don't think *I* could ever make anything," I say. "At least, I don't *feel* like I am the sort of person who can make anything. Not like that."

"Let me see your hands. Closely," says Tarni.

I hold out my hands to her, palms up. She takes them in hers.

"Yes. They are too soft. Like I said. Even though they are dirty with the outback dust and sore from carrying your case, I can see that they are not tough enough to have done much work. Not hard work." She pauses and runs her fingers over the tips of my own fingers. "Except for…" She does it again. "Except for *this* hand." She squeezes my left hand. "This hand… The tips of the fingers on this hand… They are hard. The ends of the fingers…they are hard. Why is that?"

I shake my head. "I don't know."

"The tips of the fingers on the other hand are soft. But on *this* hand…"

"Why? What does that mean? Should that tell me something about myself? I don't understand."

"No," she says. "Neither do I."

74

Tarni goes off to find some food.

"Don't go too far," I say, nervous of being left alone in this wilderness once again. "Stay near."

Tarni smiles and marches off, a small colourful dilly bag in one hand, the slingshot tucked into her back pocket.

While I wait, I throw sticks into the fire, pushing them awkwardly into the flames, trying not to get burnt. As I do that, I hum quietly in a particularly ineffective attempt to fool myself into thinking that I'm not on my own.

Not long later – thankfully – Tarni returns. Her dilly bag looks full and – oh – hanging from her hand, by their legs, are two of the wading birds.

"You killed them?" I ask, nodding my head towards the slingshot dangling out of her pocket. "With that… thing?"

"Really, Moonflower. You always ask the stupidest questions."

"Did you have to?" I feel a little sick watching the two birds' lifeless bodies swaying at Tarni's side. "I mean… isn't there something…"

She stares at me with inquisitive eyes.

"But…" I see the cage. "I don't understand. You're

happy to kill *them*." I point across the lake to where more of the birds are feeding. "So why didn't you kill *him*? Candelabra. Why didn't you kill him when you found him?"

"That's different," she says.

"How? Why is it you're happy to shoot *them* with your sling, but you built this one a cage? Why didn't you eat Candelabra?" I feel confused and angry at the same time.

"Because Candelabra doesn't belong here. He's lost. He needs to get back to the place he came from." She frowns. "I'd've thought that was obvious. But these birds – they're black winged stilts if you didn't know – they belong here. This is their home. They know what it means to live out here. They know that at any time they might get snapped by a croc or jumped on by a dingo. It's deep down in their spirit. Always has been. It's how they live. Knowing these things." Tarni looks at me like I have said something ridiculous again. "You spend too much time looking at things the wrong way," she says. "City girls like you *never* understand. You get your beef steaks all served up to you on a fancy plate with fancy knives and fancy forks. You don't care where it comes from. You don't even know what it is you are eating. You don't think about it at all."

I don't know how to reply. I want to say that, no, it's

just cruel to kill animals for food like that. That everything has a right to live safely without the fear of being eaten, doesn't it? But another part of me... Another part of me realizes that in my real life I probably guzzle down chickens on Sundays and turkeys at Christmas...all without thinking of the creatures they once were.

So, I don't say anything and try to avoid looking at Tarni as she begins to pluck the feathers off the birds.

I sit cross-legged and watch as Tarni stirs the parkily in the pot.

"Where are you going, Tarni?" I ask. "Why are you out in the bush all on your own? I mean, you seem too young to be out on your own. Whoever I am, I'm certain I wouldn't be allowed out on my own like this. Not...well, not *here*, anyway."

She doesn't say anything. I think she is pretending not to hear me again.

"Tarni?"

Her eyes look up at me.

"Where are you heading? You're not going home to Utopia. So, where *are* you going?"

She shrugs. "Dunno. Not...completely...sure yet."

"What do you mean? You must be going somewhere."

She rubs the smoke from the fire out of her eyes. "Got a good idea. But…I'll see."

I feel the panic in my chest once again. "You *are* taking me to…a town…or something, aren't you? I mean, we *are* going to a place from where I can be rescued, aren't we? Like a police station, yes? Somewhere where somebody can take me home again?"

Tarni nods. "Yeah, yeah. Don't worry about that. We'll get you back to your city. Somehow."

I relax. A tiny bit. "Okay," I say. "Good."

Tarni twists the wading birds on their skewers. "Just have to find something first." She corrects herself. "I mean…some*one*."

Someone? I think. But the stabbing look in her eyes tells me to stop asking questions, so I keep my mouth closed once more.

I dream of the pattern again. A diamond inside a diamond inside a diamond. All inside a square. Lots and lots of squares, as far as I can see.

In the dream I look down. And I see my feet. One foot wearing a smart black shoe. The other bloody and red. Both feet are standing on one of the squares.

And I realize what the squares are.

They are tiles. On a floor.

I am standing on a cold marble floor made up of diamond-patterned tiles.

It is a floor I must know well.

Then…the tiled floor grows.

It melts upwards at the edges, stretching into walls and doors and windows. Above the wide-arched doors are letters and numbers.

G1, G2, G3, G4.

I hear footsteps all around me. Shoes clipping and clopping on the granite ground. I look around but see nobody.

I hear voices. The low and mumbling voices of the invisible people walking through this high-ceilinged room.

I try looking out of one of the windows, but the dream hasn't yet managed to stretch itself into the outside world. Outside all I can see is white.

I look down at myself. I am wearing the black dress made of silk. But now, unlike previously, I have two actual shoes on my feet.

Mary Jane, I say to myself. *They are called Mary Jane shoes.*

In my hand I carry the long metal case by the handle. It feels much heavier than it normally does. My other hand reaches up behind me to feel that my hair has been put into a tight bun on top of my head.

Suddenly another voice calls out. It is louder than the other voices but the words are just as indistinct.

"Mwaw-mwaw-mwaaaw!" it calls. "Mwaw-mwaw-mwaaaaaw!"

I turn around.

In one of the doorways – one without a number above it – stands a short, round woman. She looks very old. Her face is lined and bulbous like bees must have stung it. Her nose is very red. Her eyebrows thick and slick.

She wears a dress, almost as silky and dark as the one I am wearing, and her hair is grey and curled.

"Mwaw-mwaw-mwaaaw!" She is waving to me, like I am late for something important. "Mwaw-mwawn!"

I pull the case closer to my side and race towards her. As I get nearer the dream fades, along with the old woman, and I am left standing in a desert of white cloud.

CHAPTER SIX
THE OLD MAN

After breakfast, Tarni packs away all of her things and we tidy the area in which we slept.

"Always make sure you leave no trace that you were ever here," she says.

"Why? Are you being followed?" I ask, curious.

"No. It is just a real good thing to do. When we pass through the bush we should always leave it the way we found it. That's what I was taught. We shouldn't even leave a footprint on the sand. Be like a ghost."

"That's tricky," I say, but Tarni doesn't pay any attention to me.

So, I put my new hat on top of my head, Tarni puts her bag across her shoulders, and we set off.

"Tarni," I say. "Today…could you not march off ahead of me?"

"What?"

"Well, yesterday you were always a long way ahead of me and I had to struggle to even keep you in sight."

"When you have a long distance to cover you have to walk fast," she says. "Otherwise you might not get to where you are going."

"Yes, I know," I reply. "I understand that. But today... couldn't we just walk together?"

She looks at me like I have just asked her to name every single star in the night sky.

"Well..."

"...*Please?*"

She thinks about it – or, at least, she looks as though she thinks about it – and then nods.

"Okay, Moonflower. We'll walk together. But if you slow down too much...I'll leave you stranded. Right?"

"Right." I nod and she nods back.

We stumble along, weaving our ways between the clumps of aywerte and small hillocks of red dirt – Tarni just in front and me right behind. My footprints falling precisely into hers.

As we walk, I tell her about my dream. I tell her about the hallway with the doors and the numbers, and I tell her about the old woman waving.

"You think she's your ipmenhe or your aperle?" she asks over her shoulder.

"My what?'

"Your grandmother. You think the old bat might be your grandmother?'

"I don't know," I say.

"I don't know why you bother having any of these dreams," says Tarni. "They never seem to help you remember anything."

We push on through the early hours until the sun has burst out full over the landscape and the flies are out like an air-force squadron launching an attack on my face.

As we move, I hear Tarni saying something very quietly.

"What was that?" I ask.

"Ssssh."

"Oh."

Tarni continues with her quiet words. It is like she is mumbling to herself.

I listen hard, trying to block out the sound of my own breath. I cannot make out the words she is saying, but I can tell she is saying them in a repetitive way.

Like she is singing.

We come to the top of a small hill and Tarni stops dead still.

"What is it?" I ask.

She ignores me and carries on with her low singing. She shades her eyes with her hand and scours the landscape ahead of us.

Then she points. "This way," she says and starts walking again.

As we walk, I suddenly hear a tune in my own head. Like a memory. Orchestral. Gentle. Melodic. It eases itself in with strings, I think. And flutes and clarinets join in. Soft, like a stream trickling past a lush green field. Then the strings build, becoming more persistent and dominant, but one of the clarinets raises its head above the noise trying to make its voice heard. But the strings compete harder and they fight to get louder and louder. Then, when they are at their loudest and it sounds like there is going to be an orchestral explosion...

Nothing.

My mind cannot remember the rest. Even though I sing it over and over again in my head, the next part won't come. Which is frustrating. Like everything else of mine, it is just out of reach.

We walk along a valley of sun-cracked mud and rock, dunes towering up either side of us, before slowly climbing up an even larger dune directly ahead. When we reach the top, we have a clear view of the land before us.

It is vast.

Then I spot something. Something down on the dry red plain.

"What's that?"

Tarni shades her eyes to see.

"Where?"

But there is no need to ask her again. I can see that it is moving. On two legs.

"It's a man!" I say.

"Or a woman," Tarni corrects me. "Could be a woman."

We watch for a second or two as the figure walks stealthily along, heading towards the dune on which we stand.

"They might have a mobile on them!" I say. "They might be able to get me out of here." I start to run down the dune.

"Moonflower!" Tarni calls behind me.

But I don't listen. I almost bounce down the dune towards the person, waving my free arm. "Hey!" I shout. "Heeey!"

The shape stops and looks up at me.

"Hey! Helloooo!" I reach the bottom and run towards them. "Hello!"

As I get nearer, and the sun stops blinding me, I see

85

that he is First Country – like Tarni. An old man – he looks at least a hundred – he has a massive white beard erupting from his face and a colourful woolly beanie hat tightly covering the top of his head. He wears a holey brown tank top and a pair of faded grey trousers cut at the knees with a huge tear along one leg. In one hand he holds the straps of a string dilly bag, and in the other he has a long shiny-bladed machete. On his feet he has two completely different looking shoes – one black, one green.

I stop running.

He looks quite scary.

We both stand there looking at each other for a while. Saying nothing. Then his dark brown eyes look beyond me to Tarni and he smiles.

"Ampe. Werte!" he calls out to her.

"Aywaye! Werte!" she calls back.

Tarni comes alongside me and nods respectfully at the old man. They say something to each other and the old man pats Tarni on the shoulder.

"You know each other?" I ask.

"Never seen him before in my life," says Tarni out the side of her mouth to me.

The man laughs out loud, obviously half understanding what has just been said. Once he stops, he turns to me.

"You are…like a bird that has dropped out of the sky,"

86

he says through his thick beard. "Like an arrpwere –
a magpie – that has…broken its wings."

I smile, not knowing what to make of this. "Yes." I
look down at Candelabra in his makeshift cage.

Tarni says something in her language again and the
old man says something back. I've no idea what is said
between them, but they both smile and nod and Tarni
gesticulates with her hand. Occasionally the old man's
eyes dart at me before looking back at Tarni and carrying
on with the conversation.

After a while, the old man points to a small clearing
next to a tall red rock.

"Come," he says and we follow him.

The old man sits cross-legged on the ground in the
shade of the rock and we do the same.

"Eddy," he says to me, his palm tapping his chest.
"My name…is Eddy."

Tarni says something I don't understand but I do
manage to pick out the word "Tarni" in the middle of it.

Eddy looks at me, expecting me to announce my
name, I think. I grin, unsure what to say. Thankfully I
think Tarni explains the situation to him.

Eddy looks concerned. Then he leans over, taps me on
the arm and says: "Magpie. You are magpie."

"A change of name," says Tarni to me. "No longer

Moonflower. You have now become Magpie."

Eddy pulls his beanie hat from the top of his head to reveal a curly mass of white hair. He wipes his face down with the hat before throwing it onto the ground.

"Kwarte?" he asks before taking out a small Tupperware box from his dilly bag. He prises the top off and picks out an egg. He hands it to Tarni, then he pulls out another and hands it to me.

I find myself taking it. "Er…thanks."

He lifts one out for himself and then pushes the plastic top back on. Then he cracks the shell, picking bits off and tossing them onto the ground. I can see that the egg has been hard boiled.

"Has he got a mobile?" I whisper to Tarni as if Eddy can't even hear me.

Tarni gives me one of her looks. "What do you think?"

Eddy pulls a rolled-up spotted handkerchief from out of his dilly bag and unravels it to reveal a small wooden pepper grinder. He holds the grinder above his egg and twists a sprinkle of black pepper onto it before devouring the egg in two swift bites, while I am still busy picking the last bits of shell off mine.

I see that Tarni has also finished hers and has taken the wattleseed bread out of her big canvas bag. She rips off a large chunk and proffers it to Eddy, who grins and accepts it.

Eddy says something to Tarni, who translates for me.

"Eddy says he has been to his great-great-great-niece's wedding in Ali Curung."

"His great-great-*great*-niece?"

Tarni continues. "He is making his way back home to Laramba."

"How far is that? Is it nearby? Does it have a police station?"

"It's about a hundred and eighty kilometres from here."

I nearly choke on the last of my egg. "That's a long way. And he's...well...he's not young, is he?"

"Eddy's an elder. Like any other elder in this part of the world, a hundred and eighty kilometres isn't that far for him to walk." She says something else to Eddy, who laughs out loud with a wheezy, squeaky sort of laugh.

Eddy looks at me and points to his shoes. "Shoes are no good..." I notice that the sole on the green one is practically hanging off. "... But I walk long way. Like... Superman!" He holds his arms up in the air and shows off his muscles.

"Yes," I say. "I see."

Tarni says something to Eddy, who suddenly has a

doubtful look on his face. Tarni reaches into her bag once again and pulls out her sewing kit – the one she used to make me a new shoe just the other day. She holds it up to him, her words spilling out at an unstoppable rate.

Eddy grins. "Okay." Then he removes his green shoe and hands it to Tarni. Tarni takes it and twists it about in the air, inspecting it closely, before taking a thick piece of thread out and biting it off to the right length with her teeth. She feeds it through the eye of a dangerous-looking needle and starts trying to fix the sole back onto the shoe.

As she works, Eddy talks and offers us a drink from his round water bottle.

Tarni shakes her head and I reach over to a bottle in the canvas bag. I take it out and show Eddy.

"It's okay, Eddy. We have our own."

"Ah."

Eddy takes a big swig from his bottle and I take an even bigger swig from mine.

Tarni says something, her eyes fixed on the shoe. Then Eddy says something else. This goes on a long time and – not understanding them – all I can do is bounce my head back and forth between them as the conversation plays out.

Suddenly, Eddy starts singing.

It is a low, mumbling sort of song, similar to the one that Tarni was singing as we walked. Eddy's singing voice is nasally – it is as if he is trying to accompany the words with a tune from his nose at the same time. The tune is simple and repetitive, going up then down, then up and down. Even though I cannot speak Eddy's language, I recognize the same words being used throughout.

He closes his eyes as he sings.

Then Tarni joins in. Faltering at first, like she is unsure of the song. They sing together. Eddy's voice confident and strong, Tarni's softer and less certain.

They sing the song over and over, until Tarni seems to know all the words.

Then they stop.

Tarni bites off the end of the thread, ties it all up and hands the shoe back to Eddy. He slips it back onto his foot and nods his appreciation.

Eddy looks at me. "I walk home now… Not too far."

I laugh nervously.

Then he looks at Tarni. "You go home too?"

Tarni shakes her head. "Not yet."

Eddy smiles and stands up, closely followed by Tarni, then me. He slides his colourful beanie hat over his curly hair, grabs his dilly bag by the straps once again and picks up his frightening-looking bush knife.

Tarni puts everything back into her bag and picks up Candelabra's cage.

I put my pandanus hat back on my head and take up the metal case.

No more is said between Tarni and Eddy, just a nod of acknowledgement from one to the other and back again.

Eddy turns his shiny lined face to me.

"Fly home…safe…little magpie. Kele."

Then he walks away, up to the top of the dune, before disappearing.

Not once looking back at Tarni and me.

We walk without saying very much. Now and then, Tarni breaks into her own song – almost like she is talking to herself.

"What is it with you and singing?" I eventually ask when she goes quiet again at the top of a long, rolling hill.

"Eh?"

"You sing to yourself. All the time. I don't know if you've even noticed yourself doing it—"

"Of course I know I'm doing it."

"And back there, with Eddy, you were both singing. He was teaching you a song, wasn't he?"

Tarni stops and looks at me.

"Music must be really important to you," I say.

Tarni smiles. "Yeah. Songs are important. And without certain songs, we wouldn't know our way."

"I don't understand. What do you mean?"

Tarni puts Candelabra's cage on the ground and drops her canvas bag alongside him.

"The song you've heard me singing to myself. It's not just a song. It's a map. It shows my people some of the dreaming tracks."

I lift the pandanus hat off my head and wipe the sweat from my hair. "Dreaming tracks?"

"The paths we use for travelling. You see, we don't draw our maps. We sing them. For thousands of years our ancestors have walked their way across the country. To help them know the way, they put all the important features into a song. So, a watering hole, or a real odd-shaped tree. A hill or a deadly salt pan. Things like that. Sometimes it might be the colour of the sky or a mist that gets trapped in a valley. Might be words or it might be a change in the tune or the rhythm. And as you sing the song, you name all the important things to look out for to show you that you are going in the right direction."

There is a sudden gush of wind and I have to hold the pandanus hat on my head to keep it there. We both turn our backs to the breeze to stop dust blowing into our eyes.

"Do they work?" I ask.

Tarni coughs a vicious laugh and spits sand out from between her lips. "Of course they work! How do you think my people have managed to live in this land for hundreds of thousands of years?" She shifts her position which, in my opinion, looks ever so slightly aggressive. "In the cities you use GPS. You tap a few words into a computer in your car and off you go. But what if all the computers went… *pwoof*!" She makes a little explosion sign with her right hand and fingers. "None of you would have any idea where you needed to go. You'd be lost – like you are out here. The people in the cities…they'd have to learn to read maps again – which they probably haven't done for a long time now. They'd have to try and remember how to use a *paper* map. But if those maps burn or rot or something…there would be nothing they could do. They'd be stuck for ever, lost in their shiny cities."

Tarni pulls the water bottle out of her bag and takes a deep drink. "But the First Country people…they don't rely on computers and satellites and paper books. All the knowledge they need to travel and to trade with others is up here." She taps her forehead with her fingertip. "As long as one generation passes the knowledge down to the next, those maps will always exist." She hands the water bottle to me.

I take the bottle and drink, noticing that we are over halfway through it.

"Okay," I say. "So does your…er…walking song…does it tell us where we can find water around here?"

Tarni snatches the bottle back off me and throws it into her bag.

"Nah. It doesn't. Not around here. But," she grins, "the song that Eddy just taught me does." Tarni bends over to pick up her canvas bag and Candelabra, but—

"Where's the cage?" I ask.

Candelabra and his cage seem to have vanished into the hot, thick air.

"What…?" Tarni straightens up, her face squashed into confusion. "I put him right…here. By my feet."

We both twist ourselves around, but the cage is nowhere to be seen.

Suddenly, it is Tarni who starts to panic.

"What's happened? Something's happened. Candelabra!"

"Wait."

"Candelabra!"

"He must have rolled away," I say, pointing down the long, steep hill. "That wind must have knocked the cage without us knowing and sent it rolling down the hill."

Tarni nods nervously. "Yeah. Yeah. You must be right. He's fallen down there." She takes up her bag and starts to leap down the side of the hill. "Come on! We've got to be quick."

I grip the metal case tight and pick my way down behind her.

As I get nearer the bottom, I can see that Tarni has already found the cage, wedged between two awkward, grey rocks. I watch as she pulls it out, the door dangling, no Candelabra inside.

"CANDELABRA!" Tarni screams, and the sound of her echo bounces all across the valley. "CANDELABRA!!"

"Where is he?" I call down to her.

"Candelabra!"

"Is he okay?"

"No," she shouts back up to me. "He's gone."

"He's dead?" I ask, feeling suddenly cold.

"He's GONE. He's not here. CANDELABRA!"

I stop where I am and look around. I can't see the weird little bird anywhere.

"WHERE ARE YOU?" foghorns Tarni. She clambers about the bottom of the hill, climbing over and around the rocks and bushes.

Eventually she stops and throws down the cage.

"You selfish, selfish bird!" she cries. "Go then! If that's

what you want. Go away and leave me alone." I see her wipe tears from her eyes with the back of her wrist. "In fact, you know what?... I'm glad you've gone. You were SUCH a nuisance...I always had to tidy up for you...you were so messy. I always had to look after you. You never did anything for me. So...go! At least now I'm free."

I am so shocked to see Tarni in such a state that I stay gummed to the spot.

Tarni flicks the tears off the back of her wrist and straightens herself up.

"But no doubt you'll come back again. Turn up like a bad cent. Probably won't be able to keep away, will you? Oh, no.

"I mean...if you come back...I'll make those pancakes you like..." Her voice is almost quiet now and I have to struggle to hear. "If you come back...I'll give you those beads from Ma...

"If you come back..."

She goes silent and I am not entirely certain what I should do. *Is she really just aiming her words at the bellbird?*

A slight *tipper-tapper* on the rock next to me makes me turn.

Candelabra fluffs up his wings and takes a few gawky steps towards me.

"Candelabra!" I squeal and Tarni looks up towards us. "Here he is!"

Tarni tears up the hill, snatches the bird from the rock and half throws him into the cage before ramming the little bamboo door roughly back into position.

"Don't ever do that to me again, do you hear?"

"Hey!" I say, suddenly oddly protective of the strange little bird. "Don't be so rough with him!"

Tarni glares at me. "I'm doing it all for his own good, y'know?"

"Are you?" I reply. "Are you sure about that?"

But Tarni doesn't answer, just stomps her way back to the top of the hill.

We seem to have been walking for ages (neither of us saying a word, both of us deep in our thoughts) when I spot what – according to Tarni – Eddy had called the Marriage Trees.

"Is that them?" I ask.

"Yeah," says Tarni. "I believe they are. That's real deadly, Magpie."

Two long, tall, straggly trees standing right next to each other, their branches twisting and clinging at their very top. It looks like they are both holding one another at their wedding.

"This is where I need Eddy's song and not mine."

Tarni adjusts the bag strap across her shoulder. "If you like, we're going off my grid and into Eddy's. Come on."

We cross some more wide-open desert, red as ever, before feeding down what feels like a deep valley – imposing, jagged rocks standing either side of us. Out of the direct sun, the cover of the rocks – together with the breeze channelling down the valley – feels wonderful and I take off my hat to let my head bask in the shade for a change.

The shade doesn't last long. Soon we are up again on level ground with endless sand and aywerte punctured by larger browner bushes and lifeless bent-double trees.

And all the while Tarni is singing. Under her voice. To herself. But singing. Eddy's song – I recognize it. Every now and then her eyes spot something – some identifiable point on the landscape – from the song and she indicates and leads the way.

We almost turn back on ourselves at one point and, even though for a second or two I think that Tarni has made a mistake, it soon becomes clear that it is all just a part of Eddy's song and that we are avoiding a huge crumbled-down cliff face ahead of us.

I am starting to realize that no journey in this land is ever small. All travel is done over unmeasurable hours and over great, great distances.

And. It. Is. Exhausting.

So, it is a surprise when Tarni announces – much earlier than I would imagine – "There. That's what we're looking for."

Jutting just out of the red dust is a long, wide, flat ridge of red stone. It looks like a great snake of granite that once squirmed its way along the sand only to be struck down, squashed and petrified by a giant wizard.

"What is it?" I ask.

"Well…" She lifts her hand to show me what I have already seen. "It's…it's a big strip of rock. I'd've thought that was obvious."

We walk down to where it starts and step up onto it.

"We're meant to find water on this?" I say. "On a flat rock?"

Tarni ignores me yet again. "We're looking for circles," she says. "Carved into the rock. They'll tell us where the water is."

We make our way along the edge of the granite, watching out for circles, with me secretly not expecting to find any.

"Are you sure this is the place?" I ask. "I mean, is it not possible you made a wrong turn or that Eddy's song is…um…faulty?"

"Keep looking," Tarni snaps back.

I step over some particularly sharp edges to the rock and then kick some old stones from off its surface onto the desert floor not far below.

"There," says Tarni pointing down. "There they are."

In the rock, dug in with a crude tool, a couple of centimetres thick and deep, is a circle. I kneel down to look closer. I let the tip of my finger trace round it and I can see that, whoever carved it, carved another circle inside the first, and another one inside that, so it looks a little like an archery target.

"Over here!" cries Tarni behind me and walks up to a place where a big flat slab of rock has been balanced on top of the granite outcrop. Bending over she lifts up one end of the slab a few centimetres and pushes it out of the way. Underneath it I can see a jagged hole filled with water.

"There!" Tarni stands back and admires it. "A gnamma. The one Eddy told me about."

"A well?" I ask.

She squats down on her knees and runs her fingers through the still water. The hole itself is only about thirty centimetres in diameter.

"Kinda. It's clean water – we don't have to boil it." She stands back up. "These are real important to us. They're what's kept our ancestors alive since the Dreaming."

Tarni points to the archery target symbol etched into the stone. "If you ever see a circle sign like that – circles inside other circles – it means water is nearby."

Circles inside circles. I suddenly think of my dream. A *diamond inside a diamond inside a diamond.*

And a big click happens inside my brain.

"Petrovsky."

"Eh?" says Tarni, scrunching her face up at me.

"Madame Petrovsky. That's the name of the old woman in my dream."

"So, what do you know about this...Madame Petrovsky?" says Tarni, throwing another dried stick on the fire she's just managed to get burning.

I sigh. "Nothing! I don't know anything about her apart from her name and an idea about what she looks like in my dream."

"*Madame.* Isn't that a French word? Do you think she could be French? Are *you* French? You sound pretty Australian to me."

I find myself laughing. "If I *am* French I've clearly forgotten how to speak the language. Anyway," I say. "I think Petrovsky is a Russian name. Not French. I think Madame Petrovsky must be Russian."

"That's if she even exists at all," says Tarni. "So far, your head hasn't given up too many of its secrets, and the ones it *has* given up I don't think I completely trust."

"You think my brain is lying to me? You think all the sun and heat are playing tricks on me?"

Tarni shakes her head in an "I-don't-know" sort of way.

"Do you think Madame Petrovsky might be dead?" she asks. "Because if she is you probably shouldn't be saying her name."

"Why not?" I ask.

"In my culture," Tarni explains, "once someone has died you aren't allowed to say their name. As a mark of respect. And not to disturb the person's spirit."

I think for a second or two. "What am I meant to say instead then? It's impossible to refer to someone and not actually use their name."

"First Country people have managed to do it for a very long time."

"But...I don't understand."

Tarni grins. "Sometimes we use substitute names for people when they die. We use Kwementyaye a lot."

"Ha! I can't even say that. You know, I think I'll just believe that Madame Petrovsky is alive and call her Madame Petrovsky. That's *probably* easiest."

Tarni carries on. "If there is someone in the community with the same name as the dead person, then even *they* have to be called Kwementyaye for a while to avoid saying the name."

"That's ridiculous!" I laugh again, but Tarni isn't smiling.

"Is it?" she replies. "I always thought it was just... respectful."

I stop laughing.

Later, as we finish off the rabbit that Tarni has caught, we watch the stars slowly appearing in the dimming evening sky.

"Clear night tonight, Magpie," says Tarni, jabbing her fork upwards. "Get a real good view of the stars. Be like nothing you've ever seen before in the city. Too much light pollution in the city. All that street lighting and shop lighting and stuff...stops you from seeing things that are always there."

"How do *you* know? Have you ever been to the city?" I ask.

"Me? Not often. What would I do in the city?" She picks up one of the rabbit bones in her bowl. "The cops would probably arrest me for stealing rabbits out of the parks." She bites a chunk of meat from the bone and drops it back into the bowl with her fork. "Or for kipping on the middle of a roundabout." She wipes her hands together and sets the bowl aside. "Me and cities don't mix well. Loads of people in not much space. Mobs." She makes a face. "Horrible."

"Well…you *certainly* can't say there are *too* many people out here," I say, chewing on a particularly chewy fruit. "Apart from Eddy we've seen nobody. Feels creepy to me. Like everybody else in the world has died."

"Don't worry, little Magpie. They ain't dead. Just hundreds of kilometres away sitting on their boring sofas, watching their boring televisions. While we're out *here*. Which makes them *as good as* dead in my eyes."

I try a smile before taking a swig out of the bottle that Tarni has designated mine.

Hundreds of kilometres! Oh.

I distract myself again. "So…*who* are you looking for, Tarni?" I ask.

"Hmm?" I'm not sure if she hasn't heard me or is *choosing* not to hear me.

"Yesterday…you said that you were looking for something. Then you said you were looking for some*one*." My mind jumps back to when Candelabra escaped that afternoon.

"Did I?"

"Yes. Who are you looking for? Is it your father?"

Tarni looks up at me. "Not much point looking for *him*. Don't even know who he is."

I say nothing and I watch as she puts her bowl a little further out of the way. Then she unscrews the top of her bottle and tips some of the water out onto her fingers. She does it all so meticulously – eyes focusing on the job, fingers slowly rubbing against each other – that I realize she is trying to avoid looking at me.

So, I decide to ask again.

"Okay..." I start. "If you are not out here trying to find your father...who *are* you looking for?"

"It's a long story," she says, her eyes not moving from her fingers. "You don't want to know."

"I do."

She shakes her head. "No, you don't. All you wanna do is get back to your home. You don't really care about what I'm looking for. It doesn't mean anything to you."

"How do you know?"

She doesn't answer.

"You don't have to tell me if you don't want to," I say.

Suddenly Tarni pulls Candelabra out of his cage and inspects his wings.

"That's feeling a lot better, isn't it, little fella?" she says.

"So much better." She strokes his feathers and he doesn't struggle. "Not quite there yet though, are you?"

Tarni puts Candelabra on the ground in front of his cage. We both watch him as he picks tiny bugs out of the dirt, chewing them up and swallowing them down. The amazing thing is that he doesn't try to escape. He pecks the ground and struts around in a small circle, at no time looking like he might spread his wings and fly away. Instead, after a couple of minutes of eating, he turns towards his cage and jumps straight back into it.

Tarni leans over and locks it.

"Why didn't he just go?" I ask. "Earlier today. He could have just flown away but he didn't."

"Knows the time isn't right to go yet," says Tarni. "Knows he needs me a little bit longer." She runs her hands through her thick hair, picking out a small twig that has got stuck there and flicking it to the ground. "When something relies on you – when some*one* relies on you – and you rely on them, it's not easy for just one of you to walk away. Or fly away. That was what I always thought anyway."

I still say nothing. It is like she is talking all this through to herself. So, I don't move and I let her speak.

"You would think that a bond between two people brought up in the same place together, from the same community, among the same people, would be strong enough to hold them together for ever. You would think that playing the same games, climbing the same trees, laughing at the same jokes, would glue them to each other. Eating the same foods, sharing the same experiences. You would think that nothing could ever pull them apart.

"But I've learned that that isn't always the case. Just because you walk on common ground for a while doesn't mean your footprints will always trample the same patch of dirt. Because they don't."

Tarni stops herself talking before taking another drink from her bottle. Eventually she puts the screw top back on and slides it into her bag.

Then she stares at me.

"I'm out here looking for...my sister," she says.

I watch as the darkness wraps itself all around us and I twist my neck to peer up at the stars. Tarni is correct. It is remarkable. Each star looking crisp and certain in the deep night sky. Spooling like sunlight on an oily river. Moving among them I spot the regularly flickering red light of a plane, cutting across the sky towards who-knows-where.

Who-knows-where I *am going?* I think.

I turn back to Tarni who is picking stones out of the soles of her sandals. "So, tell me about your sister. What's her name? How old is she?" I ask.

"Seventeen. She's seventeen."

"And is she as tough as you are?"

"Nah. Much *much* tougher."

Her eyes look sad. Then she turns as if to check that nobody is watching.

"Brindabel," she whispers. "My sister's name... Brindabel."

PART TWO

Rhapsody – *Music* A musical composition that is
full of feeling and is not regular in form.
(*Oxford English Dictionary*)

CHAPTER SEVEN
THE CAVE

It takes Tarni a few hours to unravel Eddy's song and to get us back onto her original dreaming track. I almost recognize the place where we diverted yesterday and even point out the direction we need to go.

We pass a crop of aloe vera plants, and Tarni cuts one of the stalks off for me. As we walk, I rub the gel into the skin on my face and arms. Holding up my arms, I am shocked at just how red and burnt I am and I only really realize how sore I have been when the aloe vera starts to cool and soothe my skin.

The day is – no surprise – hot, and I waft my hat up and down in front of my face to try and force some air over me. It doesn't really work.

I spend most of the morning trying to figure out who Madame Petrovsky is. I try to picture her face and I look down and notice the fingers on my left hand twitching.

Every now and then, Tarni stops for a few seconds, bending over and picking up stones. She turns them over in her hand – feeling them and looking at them – before either putting them into her bag or tossing them back down onto the dirt.

"What are you doing?" I ask eventually.

"Stones," she answers without further explanation.

I remember the strange stone in my own pocket – the marble – so I reach in and pull it out. I hold it up to Tarni, who stops walking and takes it.

"Boy," says Tarni and whistles. "That's a real beaut. I haven't seen one quite like that before. The only ones I ever had were tiny fellas. The usual size, you know. Clear glass with horrible bits of dark green swirl inside. Chipped. Boring. But this one…this is a real beaut. A real king. You must spend loads of time keeping it polished. What a beaut! A giant marble!"

"Yes," I say. "I think it must be important to me."

"I'm sure. You probably won it."

Then…somehow…another click in my head. From out of nowhere, another memory.

In the memory I am standing outside. Where, I am not sure, but I can hear children around me. I hear their chatter and I hear their feet slapping on concrete as they race around. And then I hear my own voice.

Give it to me, I say. *Give it to me now.*

But… It is the voice of another girl. She sounds like she is crying. *But my grandfather gave it to me. It was a present. It means a lot to me.*

I don't care about that, I say. *If it's so important you shouldn't have used it in the game. I won it. Fair. And. Square. So give it to me.*

Pleeeease! Let me keep it!

No. Come on! Hand it over! It's mine now.

Then the tiny memory fades and I find myself standing in the heat once again.

"What?" asks Tarni.

"It's a peppermint swirl marble," I say. "I…er…won it off Figgy Day." The memory has left me feeling oddly sick. *Is that really me? Am I really such a…a bully?*

Tarni squints at me. "You just remembered that?"

I nod.

"Remember anything else?"

I shake my head.

Tarni pushes the marble back into my hand.

"Why is it," she says, "that the things you *do* remember are so random and unconnected? I mean, what's the point of remembering that you won a marble from some kid called Figgy Day? Weird name, by the way."

We pick mulga apples off some trees and eat them as we walk. They have a sweet fresh taste not unlike actual apples but are much chewier and I find myself having to spit some especially rubbery bits out.

"It is a good skill to have," says Tarni. "Eating while you walk. Means you can cover big distances."

"I'm pretty sure it's not very good for you," I reply. "I'm certain somewhere in my mind I can recall being told that exercise after eating – or especially *during* eating – isn't good for you."

"Yeah, well, that's typical lazy city logic for you. Nothing more."

I don't respond.

Suddenly a flock of tiny birds – zebra finches, says Tarni – fill the sky, blurring the horizon and sweeping around like a dust cloud. There must be thousands of them.

We stop and watch as they swirl above the trees – their high-pitched chatter forcing Candelabra to respond in his own high-pitched way – until, certain that every single one of them is accounted for, they move on a couple of hundred metres out of the range of the two strangers that have infiltrated their territory.

Birds... Thousands of them...

Then…another random flash of memory.

Me, staring out of a small window as thousands and thousands of birds – just like Candelabra – swoosh past, momentarily blocking out the light. Then a rumble. Then a bang.

And that's it. Nothing more. Like slowly being handed individual pieces to a massive, complicated jigsaw, I want to shake myself hard and make more pieces drop out of the box.

Make them slot together.

But I can't. I seem to have no control over my recollections. It is as if my brain has decided how much information it wants me to have at any one moment.

Drip, drip, drip.

And it is so isolating.

And frightening.

And maddening!

The day moves, I move, the sand moves, but my mind stays still.

"You okay?" asks Tarni. "You look as if you've just seen a yowie."

"NOT REALLY," I find myself shouting. "I mean, how could I be? I don't know *who* I am. I don't know *where* I am. I don't know where I'm going. I don't know what I'm doing here. I don't know why I insist on carrying this…thing." I lift the metal case slightly. "I don't know why I've got a marble in my pocket. I don't know who Madame Petrovsky is. I don't know where my other shoe is. I don't know who my parents are. I don't even know if I *have* any parents. I don't know if I have any brothers or sisters. I don't know what I'm trying to get back to. I don't seem to know anything.

"I mean, if I can't remember anything at all…well… do I even exist?"

"Perhaps you only exist in my mind," says Tarni. "Wouldn't that be cool?"

"COOL!" I shout again. "COOL! How is that cool?"

Tarni smiles. "You sound angry."

"Well, wouldn't *you* be?"

She seems to think about it for a few seconds. "Probably. But being angry isn't going to get you anywhere."

"NOT being angry hasn't got me anywhere," I spit.

Tarni ignores me. "Anyway," she says. "There *is* something you know and that is that you are here with *me*. And I'm not going to let you come to any harm. So shut your trap and keep walking."

She takes a few steps.

"NO!" I shout.

She stops.

"What?"

"Why should I? After all I don't know where you're taking me," I say. "I don't know where we're going. We walk and we walk and we walk and we walk, but I don't know why."

"I told you why."

"To find your sister. To find Brindabel. Yes, I KNOW that. But I don't understand WHY."

Tarni looks at me like I am picking at a sore on her arm.

"THEN you say you're not sure where you're going," I continue. "And I'm worried that you're as lost as I am. I'm worried that all we're doing is going nowhere. Just ROUND and ROUND in circles. I mean, have you even been here before? How well do you know this area?"

I notice Tarni glance down at her feet.

"Not very."

"Have you ever even BEEN here before?" I repeat.

A pause.

"No." She shakes her head. "No, I haven't."

I find myself flapping my arms in consternation.

"But I know the songs," Tarni adds. "I know the songs well. In that way it doesn't matter that I've never been here before. My ancestors have been. And they show me the way. Their spirits are guiding me."

"Oh, PLEASE!" I say. "Don't go all...all...mystical on me."

Tarni's face turns into a tornado. She puts everything down on the ground and I see the muscles in her arms tense up.

"I don't think you really appreciate everything I've done for you," she says through tight teeth. "If it wasn't for me, you'd be buried under a mountain of sand by now and be lunch for a million termites.

"I made you a shoe when you needed one. I made you a hat to keep the sun off your head and face. I've found food, hunted and cooked for you. Shown you how to get water. I've kept you alive." Her eyes are wide and bright and I find I can't look at them for too long. "And all you can do is stand there in your...silky dress and tell me that the things my ancestors created – the dreaming tracks they sang into existence – they are nothing. Just...*mystical* rubbish."

We both stand there in silence for ages, the only sound being the wind, which has suddenly come from nowhere, whipping around our legs.

I feel sick.

I suddenly feel like I have said things which did not need saying. Things which make me appear ungrateful and spoilt, and I remember all the tiny little flashbacks of memory I've been having and realize…I *am* ungrateful and spoilt.

"Tarni," I say quietly. "I'm…sorry."

Tarni says nothing. She still stands there, ignoring me. She looks at the wind blowing sand around in swirls. Then she looks at the sky.

"Better get moving," she says in a tone that tells me nothing about how she is feeling. "There's a storm coming."

We say nothing as we walk along, Tarni a few paces ahead of me.

The sky gets darker and the wind gets stronger and I have to push my hat hard down on my head to stop it blowing away. I keep my eyes squashed as shut as I can to keep the sand out, and I can see that Tarni carries herself with her shoulders high and her hands wrapped around Candelabra's cage.

We force ourselves on as the gusts knock us about, first one way and then the other.

At one point, there is so much sand in the air that I can't see Tarni. I try to call out but the wind takes my breath and, anyway, the noise would simply smother out the words.

Suddenly a hand appears out of the red dust in front of me and grabs me. Desperate not to lose her again, I take my hand off my hat and clutch Tarni by the arm. Within seconds my hat is blown clear of my head, never to be seen again.

I can't see a thing. Everything is red. And I can't hear anything. The winds are too loud.

Tarni trudges on, me right behind. Sand blows into my mouth and I have to keep spitting to get it out. Sand blows up my nose and I have to wipe it with the back of my wrist to even be able to breathe. Sand blows all over my hair and my head and I feel like I am about to drown in it.

It's like I have just walked into hell.

We keep going, the sandstorm showing no signs of ending.

At one point I almost stumble, but Tarni's hand pulls me back to my feet and I manage to stop myself from falling completely.

It is endless.

And then—

Tarni pulls me past what feels like a sharp and rocky wall, into blackness and silence.

"What—?" I say.

"Sssh," says Tarni. A second or two later and a flash of light seems to fill up our faces.

Tarni is holding a small torch. She shines it into my face and blinds me.

"Ow!"

"Sorry. You okay?"

"Yes...I think so. Where are we?"

"A cave."

"That's lucky," I say.

"Not lucky at all. It's all part of the song. I knew it was here."

"Oh."

Outside the storm is blowing even harder, sand billowing in like rain through the cave opening.

"We need some *real* light," says Tarni, handing me the torch. "Hold this."

I take the torch from her and sweep the beam around the cave. It's small with dry-looking walls and jagged chunks of rock pointing inwards at us.

"Not over *there*," says Tarni. "Point it over *here*." She tuts.

I aim the torch at Tarni, who is squatting on the floor. She has taken a neat little lamp out of her bag along with a small bottle of clear liquid and a tiny rectangular box, which she shakes.

"Emergency matches," she says, grinning like she has been caught cheating at a test. She sets the matches on the ground and turns her attention to the lamp.

Tarni unscrews a cap on the base of the lamp then pours some of the clear liquid into it. She puts the cap back on and then twists a little dial on the side.

"We have to let the fuel soak up along the wick first," she says. "That can take a few minutes so you'd better sit down."

I put the case down on the ground and sit next to her. I keep the torch pointed at the lamp.

"Is there *anything* you don't have in your canvas bag?" I ask.

"Just well prepared," says Tarni, smiling. "When you've grown up in the bush you learn to be well prepared."

Ten minutes later and Tarni opens up the matches, strikes one and lights the lamp. The glow that fills the cave leaves the sorry light from the torch in the shade, so to speak.

"Hurricane lamp," says Tarni. "I think it's called that because it's supposed to stay alight even in a hurricane. Which is a bit silly because the whole thing would probably just be blown away in a hurricane. Fly off into the distance. Wouldn't help anything at all."

She twists the little dial and the whole cave lights up.

"Wow!" Tarni stands up and walks to one of the rock faces. "Look at these."

I come alongside her.

On the rocks are paintings. Ancient cave paintings. Paintings of men throwing spears at kangaroos. Paintings of trees and lizards. Paintings of the sun, the moon and the stars. Hundreds and hundreds of paintings.

"I reckon these are probably thousands of years old," I say.

"*Tens* of thousands of years old," corrects Tarni. "These go right the way back to the times after the Dreamtime when my people were the guardians of this land."

"What *was* the Dreamtime?" I ask. "You talk about the Dreamtime like I know what it is, but I *don't* know what it is."

"It was the beginning of everything," explains Tarni. "When the Rainbow Serpent awoke and made the world to her liking." She points to a painting of a long, colourful snake. *Iridescent is the word.* "She made the rivers out of her twisting tracks in the sand. She made the mountains by burying her nose in the ground. She awoke all the spirits and the creatures and taught them how to live – even us humans. And she warned all the spirits and the creatures that they had to take good care of the Earth – and of each other – otherwise she would return to remake the world without us in it. The Dreaming is where time begins and time ends. It's where there is no time." She gives me a sidelong look. "Probably a bit too *mystical* for you, eh?"

I look at Tarni. "Tarni," I say, "I am...sorry. I didn't mean to sound so disrespectful."

"Hmm...you might not have meant to. But you did."

"I didn't mean to be rude about your ancestors. I don't know where that came from."

"Don't you?" Tarni still stares at the cave paintings.

"Well...I don't know. Yes. I think, in the outside world – in my city life, if that's where I'm from – I *am* ungrateful and spoilt." I think about all the little scraps of memory I've had recently. "Perhaps that's why it all comes so easily to me. Perhaps that's how I am. Just not a very nice person."

"It would explain a lot," says Tarni with a glow of a smile.

I nod.

Outside the sandstorm is still seething.

"We're not going to get any further today," says Tarni, changing the subject. "It's getting too late."

"Shall we make a fire?" I ask.

"No way," Tarni quickly replies. "That's a guaranteed way to get us both killed."

"Oh?"

"Yeah. Either the smoke will kill us or – even worse, if that's possible – the fire makes the rock crack and the whole cave falls in on us."

"Really? Does that happen?"

"Oh yeah. I knew a kid who knew a kid who knew another kid who died because of that. It definitely happens. Not a real nice way to go."

Tarni kneels on the ground and takes her rug out from her bag. She flattens it out before sitting down upon it.

"Afraid we're going to have to manage without a fire tonight. And without cooked tucker." She takes some more things out of her bag. "Dinner is going to consist of some kungaberries, a couple of scruffy-looking bush coconuts that I picked up on the trail today and...of course...how could I forget...the...last...few... mouthfuls...of..." she builds the suspense, "this!"

She pulls out the wattleseed loaf.

My heart – and also my stomach – groans.

"Oh, no."

It is cold in the cave. Very, very cold. So we both huddle into a corner with the rug wrapped about us. It feels strange to be so cold after feeling so hot just a few hours earlier. My burnt skin almost welcomes it, but my shivering bones do not. After a while, Tarni blows on her hands to warm them up. Then she reaches into her bag and pulls out some of the stones she collected throughout the day.

"What are those for?" I ask as she lines them up on the ground, putting them into some sort of order.

"Cash," she answers.

"What?"

She ignores me and takes a small pot of black paint out of her bag along with a thin, twig-like paintbrush.

She pops the top of the paint open, dips the nib of the brush in, then picks up one of the stones. "I'm a bit of an artist myself," she says. "Bet you would never have guessed."

I watch Tarni as, by the light of the hurricane lamp, she makes a few dots and lines on the top of the stone before setting it down on the ground. I look down at it and can see that she has painted the shape of a horse. It looks like the sort of thing that has been painted on the walls of the cave.

She takes up another of the stones – the second best, I suppose – and she makes a few swirls and taps on its surface before putting it next to the first.

The outline of a kangaroo.

"They're brilliant," I say.

"Oh, I wouldn't go that far," she says. "Can hardly compete with the things that these old fellas did." She nods up at the walls. "But tourists…they love anything First Country. They love anything that makes them look like they have respect for an ancient history and culture. They love to look cool. So, a little piece of actual First Country art sitting on their bookshelf or – even better – on their coffee table where other people can see it and realize just how cool they are, is deadly."

She winks at me.

"And if I can get a dollar for each one I produce…well, that keeps me in lamp oil and slingshot elastic."

She paints on the rest of the small rocks. Sometimes animals – horses, kangaroos, snakes, birds. Sometimes people – hunters with spears, men around a fire, women carrying children. All quickly flicked and stick-like, but beautiful and evocative nevertheless.

"I'd pay fifty dollars for one of those," I say.

"Don't be daft," Tarni says. "They ain't worth fifty dollars. Anyway." She picks up the first stone with the horse on. "You can have one for free. You can put it in your pocket and it can keep that marble you won off Ziggy Day – or whatever her name is – company."

I look at myself in the mirror again, my face slightly altered in the glow of the oil lamp – the oddly flickering light catching my features differently. I know myself so well, and yet I can't even put a name to my face. I know that I see this face every day of my life. I know that I must brush this hair and brush these teeth. I know that I must wash my face and wash my hands. But I can't even imagine the room in which it might happen.

I pull my top lip up and look at my teeth again. They are very yellow. Something deep inside me shudders.

I run my finger over the scar on my cheek. It has healed but looks like it might be with me for ever. *How did I get it? What does it tell me about myself?*

I put my hand through my hair, my fingers getting caught in the knots and clumps and sand.

"Who are you?" I say out loud and Tarni turns to look at me.

"You know who you are," she says. "It's just details about yourself that you can't remember. Things like your name, they're just details really." She goes back to putting the freshly dried stones into her bag.

I wish I could agree with Tarni, but I'm not sure I can.

Tarni opens the door to Candelabra's cage, reaches in and gently pulls him out, before standing him on the flat strip of rug between us. I laugh as his head jerks left to right to up to down as he tries to understand where he is. As the light in the lamp gives the slightest of flickers, Candelabra gives a small, nervous flap of his raggedy wings and lifts himself up onto my stomach.

"Ah!" I gasp.

"Don't worry," says Tarni. "He's not gonna eat you."

The drab green bird with the orange beak fluffs himself up and, raising his good wing, starts picking away at lice or some other nasty thing in his feathers.

"Ugh," I find myself saying. "Isn't that a bit... unhygienic?"

Tarni shakes her head. "Says the girl who can't remember the last time she brushed her teeth!"

I nod.

"Wanna try feeding him?" asks Tarni, scratching around on the cave floor for something.

"Er..."

"Go on. Give him this..."

She hands me something tiny, black and wriggly and my instinctive reaction is to drop it.

But, somehow, I don't.

Instead I hold it up in front of Candelabra's head.

The bird instantly stops picking away at his chest and snatches the wriggly thing out of my fingers, making me jump.

"Give him another one…" Tarni slips a second bug into my hand.

"Here you are, Candel— Oh!" He snatches this one too.

Candelabra waddles a little further up my belly, trying to see if I have any more.

"There you go," Tarni grins. "You've made a friend for life."

"My sister was my best friend. I mean, my sister *is* my best friend," Tarni corrects herself. "Always will be."

The temperature in the cave feels like it has dropped below freezing so Tarni and I snuggle right next to each other under the rug, sharing the heat from our bodies. We lie on the flattest, hardest part of the cave floor and neither of is under any illusion of sleeping well tonight.

So we talk.

"We'd do everything together. You see, Utopia's not the easiest place on Earth to live. It's not the most exciting or deadly place on the planet. And there ain't that much money going around. Loads of people who live there live in humpies – they're basically corrugated tin sheds knocked together with old trees and bits of rubbish left lying about. Sometimes, we burn old car tyres at night for light. Loads of people are ill and people drop dead from heart problems and stuff all the time." She pauses for a few seconds before continuing. "And not many of the kids go to school."

"Do you?" I ask.

She looks sheepish. "Not often." She quickly carries on with her tale. "But the people there are *good* people. Good First Country people who respect the land and their history. They work hard and try to follow the traditional ways whenever they can. Many of them live off the stuff they get from the bush – there is only one convenience store and that doesn't sell much. So everyone tries to do the best by their ancestors. And everybody tries to get by.

"But, like I said, life there isn't easy."

I tuck the rug tight under my side.

"Tell me about Brindabel," I say, rubbing my hands together under the rug.

"She's the cleverest person I ever met," says Tarni, and she smiles as she says it. "Not school smart. But smart. *Real* smart. The kinda smart that can get you through this world safely. She knows how to cope and how to survive in the wilderness. She taught me all the stuff I know. She taught me how to start fires and hunt with the slingshot. She taught me how to pick the right fruit and bushtucker so that I don't go and poison myself and get a bad bellyache. She taught me how to sew things together and how to paint and how to make the best pandanus-leaf hats. She taught me all of it. My sister was better than any school.

"You see, we would go off into the bush together. Not far. Not as far as *this*. Nowhere near. But we'd go off for days and she would show me all the things she thought I needed to know about. The *important* things.

"And I looked up to her. I mean I *look* up to her." Tarni corrects herself again. "Always will do." She pulls her side of the rug up over the bottom half of her face to keep it warm.

"So, what happened?" I ask. "Where is she now?"

"One morning I woke up and…she was gone. Just gone. She wasn't there any more. She'd argued with Ma in the night when we should've been asleep and…well… in the morning…she'd left us. I keep trying to talk to Ma about it, but Ma won't talk." She pauses for a second or two, pulling her thoughts together. "And now that my sister's gone, all Ma says is we've got to get on with our own lives. Which isn't easy, you know. When your best friend in the whole country has suddenly just…left you."

We lie there quietly for a while, listening to the slight breeze that has replaced the sandstorms outside.

"But you can't just chase her," I say eventually. "You don't know where she's gone. This land is so vast it's impossible to just walk about and try to find her."

Tarni shakes her head. "Nah. Travellers from the North come down through Utopia. Nomads. Spiritual people. They wander all across the country with camels, sometimes stopping off at Utopia, singing songs for water and food. They remembered my sister and me from other times they'd rested there. When…when I told them she had gone, they told me that they had seen her… In the North. Along this songline that we're travelling.

"They said…they had seen her…outside a silver caravan with no wheels, hidden under some ghost gumtrees. They said that the caravan belonged to someone they called the Mermaid."

"The Mermaid?" I imagine that I am making a slightly confused face. "A mermaid in the desert?" I say and realize I *am* making a slightly confused face.

Tarni nods. "They didn't say much else."

"Who's the…Mermaid?"

Tarni shakes her head. "Dunno. Like I said, they didn't say much else. They're not real big talkers."

We both think on this for a moment.

"Did you tell your mother where you were going?" I ask.

"I didn't even tell her I *was* going. I got myself prepared and just left one morning. Over a week ago. Didn't say cheerio."

I think of my own mother – whoever she is – and hope that she is somewhere trying to find me. Quickly, I try and catch myself unawares. I try to clutch at my mother's image, I try to hear the wisps of her voice, I try to inhale her scent. *Quickly, quickly. Do it quickly. Before your brain has time to stop you. Quickly.*

But no. *Still* no. Nothing.

"So," I continue with a sigh, "your mother doesn't know where you are? Won't she be worried? Won't she try and find you? Won't she try and take you back home again?"

She laughs.

I don't push this. Instead I change the subject slightly.

"Did Brindabel teach you the walking songs, Tarni?"

"No," Tarni replies. "That was a couple of old fellas and old girls in the Utopia outstations. Elders. They taught us both. We'd take time off school…well, we'd wag off…and we'd take a trip out to where they lived. Not many of the young ones show an interest, so they were pleased we wanted to know."

Tarni's arm comes out from under the rug and feeds another bug to Candelabra, back in his cage now, and we lie there in silence for a long while.

"Tarni," I say eventually. "What if you find this caravan and this Mermaid...person...and your sister isn't there?"

She shakes her head. "Dunno. But it's the only road I have left to follow, so I'm gonna have to follow it."

I find myself wondering if I have a sister like Brindabel. Or an older or younger brother. Or even a pet bird like Candelabra. Someone I am following this road to reach.

Chapter Eight

THE RIFLE

One. Two. Zero. A pause. Five. Zero. Eight.

I am *finally* asleep on the uncomfortable cave floor when a voice floods through my head in a dream. It is a deep voice. Booming in the way that you might imagine the voice of God to boom.

And it is booming out a string of numbers.

One. Two. Zero. A pause. Five. Zero. Eight.

I don't know where I am in my dream. I could be anywhere. I might be inside or I might be outside. It is not clear. The sky might be a roof over my head. The ground beneath my feet might be water. I cannot tell. I might be flying in the air or buried beneath a mountain.

One. Two. Zero. A pause. Five. Zero. Eight.

The voice booms and it is like I am hearing it echo around the cave I know I have fallen asleep in.

One. Two. Zero. A pause. *Five. Zero. Eight.*

Suddenly a flash in front of my eyes of a face. Just for a second. No, not even a second. More like a split second. Not even that. A nanosecond.

It is the face of Madame Petrovsky. Old and covered in thick, greasy make-up.

And it is screaming in fear.

I awake. Sweating, despite the freezing cold.

I sit up hard and bring up the rug that covers us both.

Tarni stirs next to me.

"Wha'?" she mumbles in her half-awake state. "Wha' is it? I'd just…gone to sleep. What's wrong?"

The oil lamp is down to the slightest of glows so Tarni reaches over and turns the little knob to make it shine brighter, before sitting up and rubbing her eyes with the front of her palms. "What's up?"

I cannot shake the face from my mind.

So pale, so frightened.

So frightening.

"I just saw Madame Petrovsky again," I say. "She was screaming."

"So what?" says Tarni. "Weird stuff like that always happens in dreams. I used to have really awful dreams about going to school, but that doesn't happen so much now."

"No. This was worse than that," I say. "I think what I saw was real."

Tarni shakes her head. "Like I said, weird stuff happens in dreams. It's never real. Unless you were just spirit walking."

"*Spirit walking?*"

"Yeah. There are cultures all over the world that believe in it. It's when your spirit – or your soul – leaves your body for some reason and goes somewhere else. Goes travelling."

"Like an…like an out-of-body experience?" I ask.

"Kinda. But bigger, I s'pose. You might be doing it when you're asleep."

I shake my head and ignore what she's talking about, desperate to get my own thoughts across.

"Look. What I'm saying is, what if it *wasn't* a dream? What if it was another *memory*? Only, this time, it was a really bad memory. A horrible memory."

Tarni doesn't say anything. She just leans back on her elbows looking at me.

"I think you're right. I think Madame Petrovsky is dead," I say.

Tarni takes a deep breath before putting her hand into

her canvas bag and pulling out the small torch.

"I'm off for a pee," she says. "Don't have a load more nightmares while I'm gone now, will you?"

She gets up and goes out through the large, cracked entrance to the cave.

I lie down on the ground and tug the rug back over me. I look at my hands and I realize that they are trembling.

Madame Petrovsky. Screaming.

Madame Petrovsky. Dead.

The words go around my head.

Screaming.

Dead.

Screaming.

Dead.

One. Two. Zero. A pause. Five. Zero. Eight.

Suddenly the numbers come back to me. I remember the booming voice and the numbers.

One. Two. Zero. A pause. Five. Zero. Eight.

I sit up again. In the gloom of the cave the long metal case casts a low wide shadow.

I reach over to it and pull it onto my lap.

Could it be?

I push the first little dial so that a "1" is lined up in its centre. With the second, I line up a "2". Then a "0" on the third.

Moving across to the lock on the right-hand side of the handle I make a "5", followed by a "0" then an "8".

I wait for a few seconds, unsure if I'd just imagined the whole number thing, uncertain that this will lead anywhere. Then I click the locks together.

They both spring open!

And so does my mouth.

Gently, I lift the lid, easing it up until it lies against my knees. There is a slight *hiss* as it opens.

Suddenly, a flash of light bursts through the cave entrance as Tarni comes back in.

"I was thinking," she says. "Madame Petrovsky probably isn't a real person at all. Like a mirage. Just because you imagined her doesn't even mean that... Whoa! What's that?" she asks, pointing the torch at the opened case.

I turn it round so she can see.

"It's a violin," I say.

In the morning, when the light is so much brighter and we can see it better, we look at the violin again. It looks very, very old.

"So what are you doing walking around the bush with a violin?" asks Tarni. "It's not the kinda thing to help you survive, is it? You can't exactly hunt down a kangaroo with a violin, now, can you? Or dig up a water soak."

I stare at it like it is something from another planet.

"I don't know."

"Can you play it?" Tarni nudges my arm.

"I don't know. Perhaps I should get it out and try."

Tarni pulls her bag up over her shoulder and scoops up Candelabra's cage. "Well…not now. We've got a long walk ahead of us. Pack it away. We need to find some tucker."

"But—"

"Come on. Before it gets any hotter."

I watch as Tarni walks away, a sickly sense of frustration in my stomach as I slam the violin case shut.

We are both ravenous. Having missed a proper meal last night, we have thunderous stomachs. All the wattleseed bread has gone, along with the berries and seeds that Tarni collected.

Soon after we set out, however, Tarni finds a bush covered in shiny green fruit. She picks them off and fills her dilly bag.

"Looks like a fruit day to me," she says. "Hopefully we'll get some meat tonight."

The land levels out once again until it is absolutely flat and the blue sky takes up so much more space than the ground. The only hills lie behind and to the side of us. Ahead there is only a straight-line horizon. No sign at all that there was a massive sandstorm just hours before.

We plough on over the land, my feet sore and blistered, my legs tired and heavy and aching. My mind occupied completely by the violin that I carry.

Suddenly there is a sound like thunder. I look to the sky but I quickly realize that the thunder is coming from the ground to our left.

Horses. Dozens of them. Racing over the red dust. Some brown, some white. Some large and long-legged, some shorter and solid. Some old and grey. Some darker and foal-like.

Their legs pound the earth, and their heads bob, sturdy and strong. Their manes and tails sweep back in their own personal slipstream.

They gallop hard and determined not thirty metres from us.

"Wow!" I say and stop to watch. Tarni stops to watch with me. "They're beautiful."

"Brumbies," says Tarni. "Wild horses. There are loads of them out in the bush." The last few drum past us and off into the distance. "Too many of them, they reckon."

"What do you mean?" I ask.

"They don't actually belong here. All these horses," she points to where the brumbies are disappearing into dots, "are the descendants of the horses of the first European explorers that invaded this land. And there are millions of them. Well…perhaps not millions, but there are loads. And they trample important plants and stuff. So sometimes the authorities have to shoot a few thousand just to keep the numbers down. Culling. That's the word they use."

"Nasty," I say.

"Mmm. Miserable men in dark glasses with guns fly out in helicopters and shoot the horses from the air. If they don't hit them right, the horses might take days to die. Or the mares run off in a panic and leave their foals. It ain't nice."

"What's their problem? Why don't they just leave them alone? I don't understand why – when it's people who cause all these problems – it's everything else that has to suffer."

"Yeah," agrees Tarni. "I like the brumbies. The brumbies are deadly."

"*But when the dawn makes pink the sky,*" I suddenly recite.

"*And steals along the plain,*

"The brumby horses turn and fly,
"Towards the hill again."

Tarni stares at me. "You just remembered that?" she asks.

I nod. "I suppose I must have learned that in school. Poetry."

Tarni sighs. "Pointless."

We keep going for hours with only a short stop to refill our bottles from a rock well and to guzzle down handfuls of the fruits and nuts that Tarni has managed to amass. The sun burns my head and I realize just how much I miss my pandanus-leaf hat.

"I'll make you another one, Magpie," says Tarni when she isn't singing her dreaming song to herself. "An even better one."

Eventually the land starts to lift again and we are walking over small hills and along the edges of rocky cliff faces and the collapsed piles of ancient landfalls. Clumps of mulga trees stand like crowds worshipping the sky, and the occasional bleaching skeleton of an unfortunate wallaby or feral cat decorates the irregular desert.

I am singing songs of my own when I hear the noise. It sounds far off.

"Wait!" I cry and stop walking.

Tarni stops and turns to look at me. Then she hears it too.

It is the sound of an engine.

I look down at my feet and I can see that we are standing on a dirt track.

"That's a car, isn't it?" I say.

Tarni scrunches up her face to listen. "Yeah."

The noise gets louder. Steadily.

"And it's heading this way, isn't it?"

"Yeah." Tarni doesn't look anywhere near as pleased as I am feeling.

The noise is coming from my left, so I move off the track slightly and turn to await the car.

"At last. Someone," I mutter without thinking.

Tarni frowns but says nothing.

The engine roars louder. Now it is closer I can tell that it has the rattle and looseness of something old. Not a brand-new, tightly tuned machine. In fact, it almost sounds like it is coughing and screaming at the same time.

Suddenly, a rusty, dirty white Jeep bounces over the horizon and *phuts* its way towards us.

"Hey!" I wave my free arm in the air. "Stop! Hey!!"

The Jeep lurches down the track like it has no suspension.

"Hey!"

I notice that Tarni is doing nothing to flag them down.

The Jeep skids to a halt in the sand about forty metres from us and I can see that strapped across the bonnet of the van with thick, crude rope is a dead kangaroo.

The engine keeps ticking over but nobody gets out of the car.

"Hey!" I shout and, even though I know that they've spotted us, I call: "Over here!"

Nothing happens. Neither of us says anything and the Jeep just stays still, apart from the occasional shudder.

It feels quite eerie.

We stay like that for a good few seconds before—

Garrrooom-clatter-clatter.

The truck makes its clumsy way towards us.

I try to see who is driving but the sun is shining off the glass and bouncing into my eyes.

"Hunters," says Tarni, pointing to the dead kangaroo.

The car rumbles and rattles itself closer before juddering itself to a standstill, the engine hissing long after it has been killed.

I wave at the driver inside. "Hi!" I say. I can almost feel Tarni's disgust.

Suddenly the driver's door pops open and a pale, cadaverous man sticks his head out. He appears to be middle-aged, and I think he has a thin moustache but I can't be certain. If he does, it seems hardly worth the effort.

The man climbs out of the Jeep and comes round the side of his door. He is staring at us over the dead kangaroo like we are ghosts. I can see that he wears a sort of grey hunting waistcoat with lots of pockets all over it, and light sandy-coloured combat trousers.

"Mum," the man says quietly.

"Hi," I say. "Am I pleased to see you."

"Mum!" The man ignores me and raises his voice a little.

"We've been stuck out here for days now not knowing where—"

"MUM!" The man shouts hard and I almost jump like a frog.

Something in the back of the truck moans and shifts.

"Mum, come out here!" The man isn't quite so loud now. "Come and take a look at this."

The Jeep wobbles as whoever is in the back of the truck starts to drag themselves out.

"What's going on?" The muffled voice is female – I think – and rasps like someone who gargles with broken glass for fun. "What're you waking me up for? This'd better be worth it."

I suddenly realize that Tarni is standing right next to me.

"Let's go," she whispers. "This doesn't feel real good."

"No," I reply. "Not yet."

I hear Tarni sigh.

The woman in the rear of the Jeep heaves herself out through the back door and tries to straighten herself up next to the man before reaching out for the bonnet to steady herself. She looks pretty old and is as round as a rock with a face that is heavy and sweaty and red. On top of her head she wears some sort of hat. Black and leathery and shapeless with flaps coming down covering each ear. I try to work out what she is wearing on her body but it is difficult to make out, other than that it looks like some sort of dark green boiler suit with a thick belt tied round the middle.

"Hello," she says to herself. "What have we got here?"

"Oh, hello," I start. "It's really lucky that—"

"It's her!" the man hisses. "Can't you see? It's her!"

I stop talking.

"What are you on about now?"

"The girl on the news," he answers. "The. Girl. On. The. News."

The woman straightens up further and her eyes squint. "Ah!" She pulls herself round the front of the bonnet so that she can see us clearly. "Yeah. You're right. For once. She *is*. She's the girl on the news."

Tarni and I both look at each other, confused.

The woman smiles and I feel as if I'd prefer it if she didn't.

The man comes alongside her and talks to her like we're not even there.

"She's the one the cops are after. The one with the reward on her head."

"Yeah," says the woman still grinning at us. "I know that."

"What are you talking about?" It is Tarni who speaks.

They both ignore her.

"A hundred thousand dollars, that's the reward. It's all over the telly," says the man, licking his lips. I can see now that he *does* have a moustache, but I don't care because I have just heard the words "cops", "reward" and "a hundred thousand dollars" and I can't think in a straight line. "Imagine what we could do with a hundred thousand dollars." I can see that he is staring into the distance, imagining.

The grinning old woman – still watching us – replies to the man out of the side of her mouth.

"Yeah, but imagine what we could do with a quarter of a mil instead."

"Eh?"

"It's a hundred thousand *now*, sure," she says. "But the rumour is that the cops are going to hoick it up to *a quarter of a million dollar*s if she's not found soon."

"A quarter of a mil!" The man whistles.

"A *quarter of a mil?*" Tarni turns to me. "What're they yabbering on about?"

I don't answer. I can't say anything.

"Pity we found her as quickly as we did then," says the man.

The woman folds her arms in front of her and squishes up her face like she is trying hard to think.

"Okay," she says finally. "What about this. We take her back to the farm. Keep her hidden away in the cubby house for a few days or weeks – just long enough for the cops to up the cash – then hand her over. Be like real heroes."

The man nods like a rooster, a slick smile appearing under his almost invisible moustache. "Yeah. That's good. That's good. Perhaps...perhaps we could sell our story to the papers too. About how we found her. Could get another twenty grand for that."

The woman grins. "Good thinking, Bobby. Good thinking."

I see the man looking at Tarni. "Thing is...the news never said anything about *another* girl."

"Don't you worry about *her*," says the mother.

She whispers something to the man that I can't hear and he goes back to one of the open doors of the Jeep.

"Listen," I find myself saying and taking a brave step forward. "I don't know who you are but you can't just go and—"

Ka-lick.

The man is pointing a long rifle straight at me.

"Er…" I stutter.

Silence for a second, and then—

"Whadya think you're playing at, you drongo?!" Tarni shouts, her anger rolling like lava. "Put your stupid gun down or I'll pop you with one of my slingshot ball bearings. You won't be able to sit down on the dunny for weeks."

The woman laughs and the man smiles before redirecting his aim at Tarni.

"Sounds scary, kid. A ball bearing! Oh, wow! How am I meant to sleep tonight?"

Tarni and I look at each other. In Tarni's eyes I see rage. I think in my eyes she sees fear.

"Tarni," I squeak.

"'S okay," she whispers to me. "'S okay."

For some reason my frightened brain decides to remind me of the things Tarni told me about a yowie.

Some people say it comes into your house or your hut

at night and steals you. Takes you into the woods and rips your arms and legs off and eats you. Leaves your bones in a nice, neat pile...

I try to shake the terrible image from my head.

With little success.

It is then that I notice the man coming around the Jeep and standing with his rifle pointing at us, switching his aim between Tarni and me.

"But won't the kid tell the cops what we've done when we release her?" he says.

"Not if she knows what's good for her," the old woman growls. "Anyway," she puts on her frightening grin again, "I'm sure once she gets to know us, she'll understand."

"And if she doesn't?" says the man, his cheek squashed up against the rifle's butt.

"Then there are various threats that we might have to coax into existence." The woman's eyes are dark and like pinholes in her face. "Same thing goes for this one." She points at Tarni. "If she goes and spills to the cops, we'll hunt her out and..."

"You don't even know who I am," says Tarni.

"Bobby!" the woman calls. "Get that mobile phone of yours. Take a shot of the face."

"Sure thing."

The man backs up to the car door, opens it again and

pulls out a mobile phone. He lowers the rifle, leaning it against the side of the Jeep then holds up the phone, pointing it loosely towards us.

"You're not allowed to do that," says Tarni. "I'm First Country. You're not supposed to take pictures of us."

"Say cheese, girly," crows the man and takes a shot of Tarni on his phone. "There. Got you."

"Now if you *ever* try and go to the cop shop, we've got your picture. And we *will* find you. And we *will* hunt you down."

"What?" says Tarni. "Out here? In the millions and millions of square kilometres of outback. I don't fancy your luck."

"We've got friends. Lots of them. We know people. We...have...our...ways." There is something particularly menacing about the way the old woman says this that even Tarni stops answering back.

The man slides his phone into his pocket and takes up the rifle again.

"Now." The old woman slouches towards us. "My dear." She looks at me. "You're going to come with us. You...and that!" She points at the violin case and my fingers automatically tighten around the handle.

The woman holds out her hand. "Give it to me. I want to see it."

I lift the case up to my chest and wrap my arms round it. "No."

"Come on." She is still grinning. "Hand it over."

I take a small step back. "I…said…no."

"GIVE IT TO ME!!!" she shouts and I jump, my heart banging against the metal case.

"Give it to her, Magpie," says Tarni. "Just give it to her. It doesn't matter."

"Yeah, do as your friend says," says the old woman, whose grin has disappeared. "Pass it over."

With reluctance I hold the violin case out and the woman wrenches it from me. She tries to open it but seeing the locks, pushes it back towards me.

"Open it. Now."

I put the codes in and click the locks open before holding it up to her once again.

She takes it and walks back to the Jeep where she puts the case on the bonnet, next to the dead kangaroo. The man sidles up to her, the rifle still vaguely pointing in our direction.

"Let's see it," says the woman before flipping open the top of the case.

They both stand there staring at it for a while saying nothing.

"Doesn't look like much," says the man. "Just looks

like a fiddle to me."

"That's because you lack culture." She reaches into the case and starts stroking the strings. "I read about it. It's a Stradivarius. A *rare* Stradivarius too. Made during the early eighteenth century."

"What's it worth?" the man asks, rubbing his nose with the back of his wrist.

The woman turns to look at the man. "Really, Bobby. Must you always reduce everything to such *vulgar* levels?" she asks. "This is a piece of art, beautifully constructed and therefore – in a sense – absolutely priceless."

"Yeah, but what's it worth?"

"About three million dollars according to the paper."

What?

The man's jaw drops open. "No wonder the cops are trying their best to find it."

The woman unstraps the violin from its case and lifts it out. She holds it up to the light and twists it over, inspecting it.

"Beautiful!"

I can see the man's brain thinking. "The violin's worth more than the money we'd get for returning the girl to the cops." I see him looking over at Tarni and me. His eyes look dark. "Wouldn't it be better if…" He doesn't finish the sentence.

"Unfortunately, we'd never be able to get rid of the thing," says the woman, admiring the shiny smooth back of the instrument. "Even with our contacts, there's no way on God's red Earth we'd be able to sell it on. Things like this...they always get traced. Then we'd be done for. And I mean *seriously* done for. No. Unfortunately, all we can really do is have the pleasure of its company for a short while and then...let it go."

"But surely—"

"No. Bobby. This Stradivarius is not going to buy you a shiny new condo overlooking the Sydney Opera House. Forget it."

The man seems a bit annoyed.

The woman eases the violin back into the case and straps it in place. Then she lowers the lid and clicks the two locks closed.

"Okay, Bobby. Get the girl." She grabs the violin case by the handle and carries it at her side.

Bobby comes back in front of me, the rifle levelled at my face. "You heard her," he says. "Get in the truck."

"But—"

"I said get in the truck!"

Tarni steps up to him. "Why don't you go and jump into a large tub of pig fat, you blockhead!"

Suddenly the man's arm shoots out. Tarni stumbles

backwards onto the ground, sending Candelabra's cage flying. Inside, Candelabra squawks and flutters, frightened.

"Tell you what, kid," sneers Bobby. "Why don't *you* just run along home? Go back to your old folks, sit around the campfire and tell each other stories about bunyips and porcupines. Yeah?"

I lean over and help Tarni get up. She looks shocked.

"What have you got in the cage?" asks Bobby. "It's making a helluva racket." He turns the rifle towards the cage. "Perhaps I'd better put a bullet through it. Shut it up for ever."

"No!" I shout.

"Don't you *dare*, you mindless jumbuck!" says Tarni, finding her anger once again.

"Bobby!" shouts the old woman over from the other side of the Jeep. "Get the girl in the truck."

He points the rifle back at me. "Go on. Inside. Now."

I look at Tarni and she looks at me.

"COME ON!" he shouts. "Move!"

Bobby reaches over, grabs me by the shoulder and pulls me on. I walk towards the Jeep.

"Don't worry," says Tarni, and I turn back to look at her. "It's going to be okay." I see that she is doing a funny movement with her mouth like she is trying to tell me something. "Just. Keep. Your. *Head*. Down."

"Run along now, kid," Bobby snaps at Tarni. "And don't forget I've got that photo of you on my phone."

"Bobby!" The mother is sitting in the passenger seat and shouting out of the window.

Bobby prods the end of the rifle into my back as I make my way to the Jeep. Then he opens the rear door and shoves me in.

On the back seat next to me is the violin in its case, sitting on a small pile of empty Diet Coke cans and Fanta bottles. I push some of them onto the floor, which I can see is already covered in old cigarette packets and ripped up and scrunched up sheets of newspaper.

And the Jeep smells. Like it hasn't been cleaned in years. Or ever, even. I think the carpet underneath all the mess must be rotting away. If I stamped my foot hard enough, I imagine I'd be able to knock a hole in the floor.

Bobby opens up the boot and throws the rifle in before climbing onto the driver's seat.

"At last!" moans the mother. "Let's crack on."

"Yes."

Through the windscreen I can see the hollow-eyed, silent face of the kangaroo staring back. And I want to cry.

The mum winds her window down further and calls to Tarni, who is standing there with Candelabra's cage hanging from her hand.

"Remember, girl. Keep your trap shut. Or we'll come a-visiting."

Tarni pokes her tongue out.

Then she does something strange. She starts walking away. Past the car. Without looking.

"She's off already," says the old woman. "Didn't hang around long for you, did she? Didn't even wave you off," she says over her shoulder. "Not exactly much of a friend, eh?"

I'm not sure what to think.

The engine roars to life like an old man clearing his throat.

"Started first time," says the man, impressed.

"Huh. Makes a change," replies the woman.

I twist my neck to see if I can see Tarni.

She has stopped walking and is now reaching into her canvas bag.

"Okay. Here we go," says Bobby.

"Shut up with the running commentary and just drive."

The gears scrunch, the handbrake eases off and the car starts to lumber forward.

Just keep your head down.

I picture Tarni's mouth as she says those words.

Just keep your head down.

The accelerator screams and the car speeds up.

I look back at Tarni again. I can see that she has dropped her canvas bag onto the ground along with Candelabra. She is holding something in her hand.

For a second I am not sure what it is. I squint. And then it dawns…

Keep your head down.

I duck. I get my head down as low as I can, given all the rubbish on the floor.

"What the hell do you think you're doing?" asks the woman. But before I even have time to draw breath to answer—

Sssmassssh!

"Ugh."

The rear window shatters, glass falling all around me.

The car jerks dangerously to the right before slamming itself to a sudden, jolting stop, my head banging into the back of the driver's seat. The engine hisses and dies as quickly as it started.

"Bobby!"

I straighten up and see that Bobby is no longer holding onto the wheel. In fact, his head rests against it. He is not moving.

"Bobby!" his mother screams. "Wake up!"

She grabs his shoulder and shakes him but he does not

move. I can see that, at the place where his neck meets his shoulder, there is a bloody mark where Tarni's slingshot bolt has just hit him.

"Bobby!!"

She shakes him even harder. Still he doesn't move. He doesn't even make a noise.

Suddenly the door nearest me opens, making me jump.

"Come on!" cries Tarni. "Quickly! Let's go."

I grab the handle of the violin case and shuffle myself across the seat to the open door. Just as I'm climbing out, I feel a tug on the case. I look back and see the tips of the old woman's fingers catching onto it.

"Come back here!" she croaks. "You're mine."

"Oh yeah?" Tarni leans her head into the doorway and yanks the case from her. "I don't think so, you stinky old kookaburra."

We run.

Fast.

Over the open red land towards the nearest dune. Tarni with her canvas bag over her shoulder and Candelabra shaking about in his cage. Me with a three-million-dollar Stradivarius violin banging against the top of my leg.

"Come on!" Tarni shouts. "Over here."

We start to climb the dune, gravity and loose sand forcing us to slow. As we near the top—

Fizzzz.

Some sand to the right of us suddenly jumps up into the air.

I look at the place from where it jumped.

Fizzzz.

A whole load more sand leaps up a little closer to me.

"She's shooting at us!" shouts Tarni and we sprint even faster.

At the top of the dune I turn round for a moment to see, in the distance, the old woman standing behind the Jeep, the rifle pointing towards us.

Fizzz.

Luckily, she is a terrible shot.

CHAPTER NINE

THE TWO MURDERERS

For hours we run. We try not to look back because if we look back we might see the Jeep. And we really *don't* want to see the Jeep. Not ever.

We run and we run even though my feet are blistered and sore and my chest hurts. Even so, it is relatively easy for me. All I have to carry is a three-million-dollar violin. Tarni, however, has her heavy canvas bag, and her arms carry Candelabra. She holds his cage in front of her, trying to keep it as level as she can while she runs.

So, after a while, we stop and we swap. Tarni takes the violin and I carry Candelabra. As I run, I peer in at the bird through the bars of his cage and watch as he bobs up and down with each step. Normally, I think this would make me laugh, but I am too out of breath and too worried that we might still get caught.

"This is definitely the most expensive thing I've ever held in my arms," says Tarni, indicating the violin case. "In fact, I think it's the most expensive thing *anyone's* ever held in their arms. I hope I don't trip over and smash it by mistake."

Inside the cage, Candelabra starts flapping about and squawking. Sometimes he does his strange bellbird noise and I find myself hoping that Bobby and his mother aren't close enough to hear him.

We run until we find another gnamma hole where we recharge our bottles. Then we run some more. We don't really talk as we run. We just run.

Finally, as the afternoon heat begins to lessen and the sky begins to lose its deep blueness, we climb our way up a small mountain path, sharp jagged rock walls knocking us on either side as we climb up to a tiny open space, flat enough to set up camp for the night.

"This is deadly," says Tarni. "If we have a fire, the flames will be hidden by the rocks, so Professor Drongo and his mum won't be able to spot us."

I feel very relieved.

I would never choose to eat lizard, but...

"As my ma sometimes says, 'Needs must.'" Tarni gives

me my portion but I find myself struggling to manage even a mouthful.

I concentrate on the fruit.

After the rest of the pitiful supper, we talk.

"You really think it's worth three million bucks?" asks Tarni, looking at the violin sitting in its open case. "No. Don't answer that," she says, grinning. "I know what you're gonna say. You're gonna say, 'I don't know.'" She whistles as she tries plucking one of the strings. "Three million bucks is a load of cash for just a tiny musical instrument, don't you think? I mean, three million bucks...well...that kinda money could buy a whole load of stuff in Utopia. Anywhere."

"It seems like a lot of money," I say.

"It *is* a lot of money."

"So, what am *I* doing with it?"

We pause to watch an eagle circle up above us before flying away.

"They said the police were after me," I continue. "They said that the police were after me and that there was a reward for my capture."

"A hundred thousand bucks," says Tarni. "Perhaps I'd better just hand you over and claim the reward for myself, eh?" She smiles as she runs her finger around the inside of her food bowl.

Unfortunately, I am thinking too hard to notice the smile properly.

"But can't you see?" I say. "I'm wandering around in the middle of nowhere—"

"Erm, you mean the middle of *the bush*, don't you?" Tarni corrects me. "*Not* the middle of nowhere. This isn't just *nowhere*."

"Okay. I'm wandering around the middle of the bush with a three-million-dollar violin. The police are so desperate to find me that they've placed a one-hundred-thousand-dollar reward on my head. Can't you see?"

"See what?"

"Well…I would have thought it was obvious."

"Hmm?"

"Well…I must have *stolen* the violin. I've stolen the violin and, somehow, in my escape, I've managed to lose my memory and find myself *here*, in the middle of… the bush."

Tarni says nothing.

"In fact," my eyes go wide, "I think I must have stolen it from Madame Petrovsky. Yes. That makes sense. That's why I keep dreaming about her. Madame Petrovsky sounds like the sort of person to have a three-million-dollar violin, doesn't she?"

"Does she? I wouldn't know."

Suddenly the pit of my stomach drops to below ground level.

"Oh no," I say.

"What?"

"I dreamed about her screaming."

"So what?"

My hands clutch at my filthy dress.

"What if I killed her? Deliberately or by accident. What if I killed her to get to the violin?"

In the darkest black of the dead of night, Tarni nudges me in the stomach. I'm surprised, not because I was asleep, but because I thought *she* was.

"What is it?" I ask.

"When you were in the back of the Jeep today…I mean yesterday. When you ducked."

"Yes?"

"When I shot the bolt through the window and hit Professor Drongo on the back of his nut. When I dragged you out of the truck."

"What are you on about?"

She pauses. There is clearly some idea in her head that she's struggling to express properly. "When the truck ran off the dirt track. Did you see him?" she asks.

"Who? Professor Drongo?"

"Yes."

"I…er…I suppose I did."

"What did he look like?"

I twist myself round under the rug and try to see her face. She looks worried.

"I…I don't know. There was a lot of blood coming out of his shoulder from where you shot him."

She doesn't say anything, so I try to carry on.

"Erm…I think you must have knocked him unconscious. He'd slumped over onto the steering wheel. He wasn't moving."

"Was he breathing?"

I try to remember. There is so much stuff inside my head that I cannot remember, and this appears to be another one of them.

"I don't know," I confess.

"Was he making any noise at all? Anything?"

"Um…"

"Any movement? Anything?"

"Like I said…he wasn't moving."

Tarni slaps the hard ground next to her.

"What is it, Tarni?"

She slaps the ground again. Even harder this time.

"Don't do that," I say. "You'll hurt yourself."

"Yeah, well, I probably deserve it, don't I?" She sounds angry.

"Why?"

"I killed him, didn't I? I shot him in the back of his nut with a slingshot bolt and I killed him."

Neither of us says anything as the sun smudges itself slowly into the early morning sky.

CHAPTER TEN

THE GOLDFISH

The next day passes like a mist. We walk onwards through the desert, this time carrying much more weight than before.

The weight of guilt.

We don't talk too much. We both have a lot to think about. However, sometimes, when we rest, I try to console Tarni.

"You know," I say. "I think I *might* have seen him move. It was only small but…he *might* have moved."

But Tarni shakes her head and waves the idea away like a dust cloud.

"I hunt with the slingshot. I kill things every day with it. If I can kill birds and rabbits and lizards with it, I don't see why I couldn't kill another human being. It's a dangerous weapon. And I've been reckless."

At other times, it is Tarni who does the consoling.

"You don't look much of a thief to me," she says. "I've met some thieves and they don't look like you."

"Oh. How does a thief look?" I ask.

"Well...not like you. You haven't got the...the look of a thief. It's not in your eyes."

"Perhaps my memory loss just makes it *look* like I don't have the look. Perhaps, in truth, I've just forgotten."

"That doesn't make sense," she replies.

"Nothing makes sense to me," I say before picking up the violin case and carrying on. "Nothing."

Some days go by. I lose count. We walk. We rest. We walk some more. We set up camp. We start a fire. We gather fruit. We gather seeds. We purify water. We hunt for rabbits and birds – well, Tarni hunts for rabbits and birds. We cook the food. We sleep. We awaken. Then we walk again.

I don't notice the landscape now. I don't notice if the next kilometre looks different to the last kilometre. I don't notice if we're walking uphill or down. I don't even notice the pains in my legs and my feet.

Because all the time I am walking, I am worrying. Worrying about the words that float around my head like corks bobbing in a river.

Thief.

And worse...

Murderer.

"Even if you *did* steal the violin – which I'm sure you didn't," says Tarni as we take shelter from the sun under an overhanging rock face. "Even if you stole it, the only thing connecting you to this Madame Petrovsky are your weird dreams. I'm sure she doesn't even exist. She's just a...figment – I think that's the word – of your imagination. The result of some nasty knock on your nut."

"But they seem so real."

"Movies seem real. But they're not," says Tarni. "They're just made up. And Madame Petrovsky's just a movie inside your own head. That's all. She's not real. So, you can't kill her. Not like...the man. He was definitely real."

"He was unconscious," I say. "That's all."

"Yeah. Right," she huffs.

It is a dull and cloudy day when we come to the road.

A real road this time, not just a dirt track. A real road made of tarmac and stone. A real road where real cars zoom along at a hundred kilometres an hour and overtake other real cars if they are fast enough.

A road.

It feels strange to see a road here. In the middle of the endless red desert. It is like someone has just come along and unravelled a strip – like Sellotape – and stuck it to the earth, before pinning it fully into place with long white staples along its centre.

"Where does it go?" I ask as we come down to it.

Tarni points in one direction. "It goes, over *there*..." Then she points in the opposite direction. "...and it goes over *there*."

"Very funny."

"Who knows where it goes?" she says. "And who cares?"

I look along the road. There are no cars and no trucks to be seen. It is utterly empty.

"It's very quiet," I say.

"Loads of roads out here are very quiet." Tarni smiles. "People with cars don't tend to want to come out to these faraway places. They'd rather race their cars around the backstreets of the cities, and park up in front of a beach or something."

I stare off into the distance expecting to see a car.

"What's that?" I ask.

"What?"

"That," I say.

"That?" she says.

"Yes," I say.

Tarni squints. "That's a gas station," she says.

"Oh," I say.

We both stand there for a minute not actually saying anything.

Tarni breaks the silence. "I suppose you want to go there. Get the people who work there to call for help. Get your ma and pa to come and get you. Am I right?" She doesn't sound delighted.

I don't know what to think. Only two or three days ago I would have said yes. I would have jumped up twenty metres into the air at the chance to be taken to a town, to find out who I am.

But now I am not so sure.

"No," I say. "You're not right."

Tarni looks surprised. "But this is the perfect place to get help for you. Just make a phone call and you can be out of here in a couple of hours."

"No."

"Why not? Because of all this 'murderer' cobblers? Magpie, you're not a murderer. *I* might be, but you're definitely not."

"I don't want to go back," I say. "Not yet. Not until I've remembered more stuff. I think I need to remember more stuff before I go back. I want to be *certain* of who I am. I want to be certain of what I have or haven't done. I want to know – completely and truthfully – what has become of Madame Petrovsky. I want to know what this violin means to me." I shake my head. "I *need* to remember."

Tarni puts on a painful grin. "That's going to take for ever at this rate. Your memories ain't exactly gushing back like a waterfall, are they?"

"Perhaps not. But I think I want to stay with you. For now. Until things begin to start slotting into place."

"O...kay." She is trying not to look pleased, but she is failing badly. "Maybe we can find the Mermaid together. Yeah?"

"Maybe."

"Yeah," she says. "That'd be good."

The road is still empty. I have a feeling it has been empty for a very long time. The tarmac looks new and smooth and straight – like there's not been enough traffic to wear it away. No potholes or skid marks. Just a slick and even grey.

"So, you don't want to pay a visit to the gas station?" asks Tarni.

"No. I don't think so."

"They might have newspapers. We might be able to

read all about you. Find out what a criminal mastermind you are."

I suddenly feel sick and don't know what to say.

Tarni turns and reaches into her canvas bag. "Thing is…a gas station is an ideal place for…these!"

In her hand she holds one of her painted stones.

"I've sold loads of these to gas stations before. They keep them on the counter so that people filling up their trucks can buy one for their coffee table. The lucky city folk don't even have to go out of their way to get their First Country artefacts. They can just pick them up along with their cigarettes and chewing gum."

"You're not going in there, are you?" I ask nervously.

She puts the stone back into her bag. "If you like, you stay here with Candelabra." She hands me the cage. "I'll see if I can sell them any of my magnificent works of art. And I'll be back soon."

She gives me a wink and turns away, walking along the side of the road towards the gas station. I watch her as she gets smaller and smaller, disappearing into the heat haze until I can't see her any more.

With Tarni gone, I remember how silent it can be out here on my own. All I can hear is the breeze blowing across the ground and around the trees, the far-off call of some bone-picking bird, Candelabra nibbling lice from under his wings (again!) and the shallow puffs of my own breath. Nothing else.

It feels eerie. Almost ghostly.

I move a little further back from the road and sit down in the shade of a gumtree. I put Candelabra down on one side of me and I lower the violin down gently on the other. I treat the violin much more cautiously now that I know what its real value is. No more bashing the locks with a big rough rock.

With my back against the tree, I sing snippets of music to myself until I begin to doze and dream.

In my dream I see a cat – a white cat with a grey face, grey pointed ears and a fluffy grey tail. Its eyes are watery blue and I can almost hear it purring in my ear.

I reach out to stroke it. It feels soft and warm.

Persian, I think to myself. *This is a Persian cat*.

It jumps up onto my lap, turning itself round in circles trying to find the most comfortable position in which to sleep. It purrs and purrs as it pulls its claws in and out of the jeans I am wearing, snagging the material.

Her claws, I realize. She is a female cat. Round her neck, she wears a gold-studded collar.

Finally, she settles, curling up snug and warm on my lap. I stroke her over and over again. It soothes me. Feeling her cosy and restful against my legs.

"There, there," I say. "Close your eyes now. Sleep well, Violet Crumbles."

I suddenly wake, my own eyes struggling to cope with the brightness of the day.

"There you are." It is Tarni's voice. "I wondered where you'd got to."

I shade my eyes from the sun and look up at her. "Did you sell your stones?" I ask, trying to wake myself up fully.

"Yeah. Ten of them. Ten bucks. Not bad, eh?"

"Excellent," I say, starting to lift myself off the ground.

My eyes adjust to the light and I can see Tarni staring at me. Scrutinizing me almost.

"What's wrong?" I ask.

She shakes her head. "Oh, nothing. Nothing." She picks up Candelabra, turns away and starts walking. "I just didn't know where you'd got to, that's all."

"Thought I'd rest in the shade," I answer. "I spend so much time out in this sun, I just thought I'd have a break. Hide away from it. And I had a dream."

"Not another one," says Tarni over her shoulder.

"I think I've got a Persian cat," I say. "Called Violet Crumbles."

Tarni stops and twists round to look at me. "You named your cat after…a chocolate bar?"

"It looks like it."

Tarni's mouth falls open.

"What's the matter?" I say. "It's not such a bad name. You named your bellbird after a light fixture."

She shakes her head again. "It's not that," she says, putting her right hand deep into her canvas bag. "It's just that…with two of the dollars I got from the gas station, I bought us these…"

She pulls something out of the bag and throws it to me.

It is a Violet Crumble chocolate bar.

We eat the bars quickly – the chocolate melting on our lips as we do so. It takes a few large swigs of the water to wash my teeth clean afterwards. When we finish, Tarni takes the wrappers and folds them carefully together before pushing them into the bottom of her bag.

"Can't leave these out here," she says. "This is sacred country. We can't spoil the land."

"Your ancestors wouldn't approve," I agree.

"No. They wouldn't."

We walk on until the road is nothing more than a dry stick lying across the landscape behind us, and the gas station not even a pin.

"Were there any papers at the gas station?" I ask Tarni.

"Nah," she says.

"So, you didn't find out anything about...me? Or you?"

"Nah." She coughs before spitting a thick blob of phlegm onto the dust. "What I did see though..." she starts.

"Yes?"

"The woman behind the counter. She was short and as thin as a wire. Her face looked like an apricot that had been left out in the sun for too long. Wrinkled and all covered in folds. Her hair stuck right up. It was curly and blonde – the sort of blonde you have to stick your head in a tub to create – and all stuck up. It was like her hair didn't want anything to do with her and was trying to get away. Escape."

"Ha!" I laugh at the image.

"And her shoes... You should have seen her shoes. Sandals I suppose they were. Brown strappy things. Dirty. But in their heels... Fish."

"Fish?"

"Yeah. Fish."

"What? Real fish?"

"Nah. Of course not. *Dead* fish. Dead goldfish."

I look at her. "She had *dead goldfish* in her heels?"

"Well, I suppose they might have been plastic.

Pretend. But the heels were clear and you could see them. I liked the look of them. They were deadly."

"You saw this woman's sandals behind the counter?" I ask in disbelief.

"Of course I didn't. Tsk! She had to come *round* the counter to see my works of art. That was when I saw them. They were cool."

I smile but, somehow, I can't help feeling that Tarni seems distracted.

"Are you okay?" I ask.

"Don't be silly. Of course I am. C'mon. Let's go."

"What will you do when you find Brindabel?" I ask before correcting myself. "*If* you find Brindabel?"

Tarni stares at me as she walks.

"I dunno. I dunno what I'd do."

"I mean, she might not want to go back to Utopia with you," I continue.

"You don't understand much, do you?" Tarni's face looks both angry and sad at the same time.

"You thought you knew her, but you were surprised when you woke up one morning to discover that she'd left."

Tarni squeezes her eyes together and glares at me. "What're you asking all these daggy questions for?"

"I don't know," I say. "But shouldn't you be asking yourself these questions? Shouldn't you prepare yourself for not actually finding her? Or her not wanting to go back with you?"

"Oh, shut your beak, Magpie." She pulls her bag tighter over her shoulder and marches on even faster.

CHAPTER ELEVEN

THE LOWERCASE LETTER R

The landscape starts to change. Even with all the worries swooping around inside my head, I can recognize this. The red dust and aywerte give way a little – just a little – to patches of grasses that sway in the hot breeze, and gumtrees greener and heavier-leaved than before.

"This must be wetter country," says Tarni. "There must be more water stored underground. If we get desperate, we can probably dig up a soak. Get water from that."

We don't get desperate though, because the day after we cross the road we come across a small creek. Not exactly a wide and deep-flowing river, rumbling its way across the land to the far-off sea, but a thin, shallowy trickle, gurgling over its rocky red bed.

Excited at such a sight, I convince Tarni to join me in stripping off down to our underwear and jumping in, splashing each other with the cooling fresh water. We clean all the dirt and grit and sweat off us, and Tarni buries her head in the stream, brushing all the dead twigs and dust out of her hair. So I do the same. It feels wonderful. It feels cathartic.

For hours we just sit and lie in the flowing water, letting it wash all over us and, for this short while at least, it feels as if the guilt has trouble sticking to our skins.

"This is nice," says Tarni, her arms moving back and forth under the gentle current. "Much nicer than sitting in a stinky old kangaroo's watering hole."

"I never want to leave this place," I say. "I think this must be heaven."

"*All* the outback is heaven," replies Tarni. "I'd've thought you would have understood that by now."

Tarni makes me a new pandanus-leaf hat. This time she ties on strips of grass with spiky gumtree pods on the end of them so that they dangle down and keep away the flies.

"The swagmen who used to travel around looking for work at the cattle stations tied corks to their hats instead," she says. "But corks are tricky to find out in these parts – not enough empty wine bottles lying around – so you'll have to make do with gum seeds."

The new song that Tarni sings to show us the way is pretty, I realize, and soon I am singing it along with her. I do not know what the words mean, but the sounds are soothing, and I find it reassures me.

There is a throbbing in the air. Far off. We stop and we listen. It is getting louder.

Something I have come to understand about being in this landscape is that you usually hear things a long time before you see them.

"What is that?" I ask.

Tarni doesn't answer but listens even harder.

Suddenly her eyes go wide and her mouth twists.

"Helicopter!" she says. "There's a helicopter coming this way." She listens again. "No. It's two helicopters. Or even three."

I clutch the violin case.

"What are we going to do?" I say. "Are they looking for us?" I feel the panic rising once again. *I still need time to work out who I am*, I think. *I need to work this all out myself. I don't want to go to prison.*

Tarni looks around. "Quickly! Over there." She points towards a big, round, fat bush and she starts running. I follow behind.

The bush is thick and spiky, so Tarni pulls her bush knife out of her bag and starts chopping at it. Large chunks drop onto the earth, so I kick them away. Tarni slashes with her knife, making a hole in the bush.

The throb of the helicopter blades gets louder and louder. I look to the sky but still can't see them.

"Faster!" I shout at Tarni. "They're coming for us!"

"Jeez! I'm going as fast as I can." She wipes her brow with her wrist.

Tarni cuts some more away before reaching in and ripping out a loose section of the bush.

"Quickly! Get in!" she says, and I clamber in on my knees, pulling the violin in behind me. "Come on! Budge up!" Tarni pushes at me and I squeeze in further, my arms scratching themselves against the dark, prickly brambles. I turn round so that I can see out of the hole. Tarni sits just in the gap with Candelabra's cage on her lap. We both stare out at the sky.

The throbbing fills the air.

Suddenly three helicopters zoom over the horizon, one after another, as if they've been spat out from the earth. Shiny black helicopters with black glass windows. They seem to lean forward as they fly, like they are scouring the ground trying to find something.

Trying to find us.

Tarni and I try to pull ourselves further into the bush as they get nearer. I hold in my breath.

As they approach us, I can see the dust from the ground stirring up into the air, like waves behind a boat.

The helicopters look cold and lethal. Sleek, black killing machines. I imagine the men inside pointing guns out of the windows and shooting down the brumbies.

I hug the violin case close, and Tarni speaks soothing words to Candelabra.

I feel scared.

Not yet, I say to myself. *Not yet*.

The noise becomes almost unbearable, so I shut my eyes and cover my ears with my arms. I pray for them to go away. I pray for them to not see us. I pray. Who to I am not sure.

But I pray.

I feel Tarni's hand clutch at my arm.

The banging in the air reaches a peak. A noisy roar. And then...

It starts to fade. Like they have passed overhead. Like they haven't spotted us. Like they missed us completely.

I open my eyes and look at Tarni, who seems to be grinning.

But all I feel is a sickly sense of relief.

After a particularly bad night's sleep, we find we are both ridiculously hungry. Setting off, we look for fruit or seeds to eat on our way. But we find nothing that Tarni recognizes as edible.

"This isn't really my land," she explains. "It's not really my country. I don't know these plants and trees. I don't know what's real good to eat and what's real bad." She licks her dry lips. "I wish I'd bought some pizza slices and some bags of chips at that gas station now. Not just some stupid chocolate bars. I was too distracted by the p… plastic fish."

Our weak legs push on, carrying us further over the land.

After a couple of hours, we come across a long cluster of bushes, short and squat but rich with fruit. Tarni goes up to one of them and picks off a little pink ball. She holds it up for me.

"Do you think that looks like a wild peach?"

I find myself pulling a funny shape with my mouth to say *I don't know.*

Tarni looks harder at the bushes. "I *suppose* they're a bit like kawantha trees. Bit shorter. Leaves not so long and pointy." She squeezes the pink ball between her fingers. "The fruit feels the same way a wild peach feels."

She's weighing it up in her mind.

And then she takes a small bite.

"*Is* it a wild peach?" I ask.

Tarni doesn't answer for a minute as she assesses the fruit. "Yeah… Nah… Maybe… I'm not sure… Could be."

"Is it?"

"Well…it *tastes* a bit like a wild peach." She takes another bite and another before tossing the stone in its centre away. "It must be. Yeah."

We pick as many of the wild peaches as we can, stuffing them deep into Tarni's canvas bag and deep into our pockets. As we walk, we eat. We bite off the flesh and drop the stones, like Hansel and Gretel laying a trail.

We cross a salt pan – the ground beneath us white, even and flat – before the desert turns red, green and black again, rising gently upwards towards the sky. As we climb, I suddenly feel a churning in my stomach.

"Go behind that tree," says Tarni, pointing to a scruffy stick of a bush. "I won't look."

I rush behind the tree and do what needs to be done.

"Better?" asks Tarni.

"I think so."

But a few hundred metres on, the churning starts again. Along with a bilious sensation in my chest and my throat. So, I rush behind another tree and do something even worse.

When I've finished and I come back round, I can see that Tarni has been sick. She is bent over like a lowercase letter r, her hands clasped to her stomach.

"Tarni?"

But she doesn't answer. She just throws up some more.

The sight of her throwing up onto the rocks at her feet, makes my stomach churn further, and suddenly I am throwing up too. Red juice gushes out from my mouth onto the dust, some of it landing onto my odd shoes. I heave and I heave, scarlet fountains arcing each time, until I feel like I've emptied my stomach out completely. Straightening up, I wipe the acidic vomit from my lips and the water from my eyes.

"You know, I don't think they were wild peaches," I say to Tarni.

"I think you're right," says Tarni, taking a swig from her bottle, swilling it around her mouth and then spitting it out. "Hopefully we didn't eat enough of them to get *real* ill."

But she is wrong.

We walk on – weak from hunger and shaking with nausea. I watch Tarni in front as she drags her feet over the ground, her fingers clutching Candelabra's cage. Where she once marched on swiftly, she now staggers and sways, stopping much too often to drink from her bottle.

I dive behind too many trees and struggle to keep the wave in my chest down. The inside of my mouth is drier than the desert floor, but I try to resist the desire to drink as much water as my body tells me it needs.

"If my sister was here," Tarni shouts back at me. "She'd know what to do. She would...know what those fruit were. If my sister was still around...we wouldn't be going to the dunny all the time...and chundering like river gods. We'd be...we'd be..."

She doesn't bother to finish.

I feel so unwell. My body is heavy. My legs shaky. My stomach like a car wash. Even though I wear my new hat, the sun feels like it is trying its best to burn me out of existence today. Frazzle me. I stink. My breath is shallow. My head banging like a car door.

I suddenly realize that this was the way I felt just before Tarni found me all those days ago. But Tarni cannot help me now, because Tarni is the same. Tarni is unwell too.

"There's another...waterhole somewhere," she says, showing me her empty water bottle and pointing pathetically into the distance. "A few kilometres...I think. Not...far. Need to get to water. When...we get there... we'll be okay. We can drink loads. Might...catch a couple of mandidi fish... Yeah."

We drag our way over a ridge towards a large clump of green-leaved trees.

"Not far…" says Tarni, her voice faint and rasping. "Not far now, Magpie."

I can't answer.

I make myself walk.

…*right, left, right, left, right, left, right, left, right, left, right…*

I feel the blood in my body. I can feel it rushing through my veins. I can hear it too. Thundering. Roaring. Like it can't stop. It feels like it is getting faster and faster and faster. It *sounds* like it is getting faster and faster and faster. I can't control it. And I panic because I can't control it. I panic because it is out of control.

It is out of control.

It is out of control.

It is out of control.

I *am* out of control.

I panic. I want to scream. I want to punch at the air around me. Swat all the flies away. Make a hole in the world.

And then my vision turns black and I feel myself falling forward.

An arm slides underneath me. Then a second. Suddenly I am carried up into the air – like the angels have come down from above and are collecting me, scooping me up in their celestial wings and taking me into their too-blue sky.

I float, swaying in the air. I feel so light. A leaf on the breeze. Blown over the land.

There is no panic in my chest now. No fear. Just a sense that I am safe. I don't need to worry. I don't need to think. There's nothing I need to know.

Everything is going to be fine. Everything is as it should be.

I open my eyes for a second – *the splittest of seconds* – before slipping into sleep.

On one of the arms that carries me, I see a mermaid.

CHAPTER TWELVE

THE MERMAID

Soft.

It is the word that I think of first when I awake.

Soft.

Everything around me is soft.

And cool.

That is the second word I think of.

Cool.

Soft and cool.

I don't want to open my eyes. I just want to lie here and feel soft and cool for as long as possible. I want to feel snug and comfortable and cushioned and cosy for ever.

I yawn.

"She's awake!" a voice shouts quite near me, and my eyes flick open in response. "She's awake!"

It is Tarni. She is standing over me.

"Morning, lazybones!" She speaks too loudly at me. "Hope you had a good sleep. We were worried about you for a while then."

"What?" I say weakly.

I look around. I am lying in a bed covered in sheets and patchwork blankets. My head has been resting on plumped-up feather pillows and satin cushions.

"Yeah. You were a real worry," Tarni smiles.

On the wall next to my bed I see framed photographs. Pictures of stern warships and submarines. And glittering medals on wide, silky ribbons are pinned alongside them or hooked over their corners.

The room I am lying in is not big, I realize. Just behind where Tarni stands is a neat chest of drawers, a tiny window above it. Not far from my feet is a small sink with a cooking unit next to it. And beyond that, some seats against the wall – under some more windows – around a wooden table. A door to the outside lies wide open.

"Where am I?" I ask, sitting myself up in the bed. "What happened?"

"You got sick," says Tarni. "We both did. Stupid peaches. You collapsed. So did I. Luckily we were close enough."

"Close enough?" I shake my head. "To where?"

Suddenly I remember the mermaid carrying me. "The Mermaid? This is the Mermaid's caravan, isn't it?"

Tarni does a half nod. "Yeah." She grabs my arm. "I wasn't well, but you *really* weren't well. I think my belly must be stronger and thicker than yours. All those years eating lizards and stuff probably turned my guts into iron. I got better yesterday. But you were still asleep. You didn't want to wake up. We gave you water, and you'd lap it up like a cat – like Violet Crumbles, remember – and you didn't wake up. But now –" she squeezes my arm – "you're awake."

I feel exhausted. I feel like all I want to do is roll over and fall back to sleep. But Tarni's excitement at seeing me awake makes me feel like I should be getting up.

"I was chundering a lot," says Tarni. "I left a lot of mess on the carpet, I'm afraid. But I'm better now. What're you doing?" She watches me pull the sheets off.

"I'm getting up," I say.

"Don't rush."

"It's okay." I swing my legs round and put my feet on the floor. I feel softness under my toes. Looking down at myself I can see that I am dressed in a far too large T-shirt that falls to just above my knees. On the front of the T-shirt is a picture of Elvis Presley. "Where's my dress?" I ask.

"It's drying. On the line. It's been washed. And I fixed it for you. The hem was hanging off, so I've sewn it back on. It's not as good as it should be, but it'll do."

"Oh." I feel oddly relieved to know the dress is still around. "And what about my shoes?" I wriggle my toes on the softness beneath. "Where are my shoes?"

"Don't worry about them. Debonaire has some old ones that you can have instead."

"Debonaire?" I ask, my face wrinkling with the question mark.

"The arelhe who owns this caravan," replies Tarni. "The Mermaid."

"Ah." Then I remember. "The violin? What about the violin? Is it safe?" I say anxiously. "You've kept it safe?"

Tarni points to the table by the window. On top of it sits the violin case.

"Okay." I nod. "Okay. Good."

I wouldn't want to lose it. That would be wrong. If I *have* stolen it, then I think I want to return it myself. Eventually. Once I'm certain of everything. Once everything's definite. Once everything's solid again. So it needs to be safe.

Suddenly a small, brown and white panting dog rushes in through the open door – its tongue flopping out of its mouth – and jumps onto the bed next to me, its tail flapping like a bird's wing. It sniffs at me and jumps up on my arm trying to lick my face.

"Hey!" I shout, pushing it down. "What are you doing?" But it keeps trying to jump up on me. "What on…?"

"That's Dog," says Tarni.

"Doh! I *know* it's a dog," I say, holding the furry beast at arm's length. "How stupid do you think I am?"

Tarni ignores my sarcasm. "Nah. That's his name. Dog."

"Not very inventive," I say, my hand getting covered in slobber.

"Yeah," agrees Tarni. "Not like *Candelabra*. That's a deadly name." Tarni grabs the dog and pulls him to her chest. "But he's a good dog." She nuzzles her nose against his head and strokes his back. "Aincha, boy?"

The dog licks Tarni's face, and she happily takes it.

"I thought you didn't think of animals as cute," I say. "I thought that all you did was eat them or save them."

"I can make exceptions." Tarni smiles.

"Is Dog annoying you?" A voice comes from the doorway and a figure blocks the sunlight that was previously pouring in. "Just shove him off the bed if he is."

The figure steps into the caravan and stands alongside Tarni.

"Good to see you up at last," says the woman with the mermaid tattoo on the arm that she extends to me. "I'm Debonaire. Nice to meet you."

I take her hand and shake it. Her grip is strong and I can see that, as well as the mermaid tattoo, the arm is covered in hard muscle.

"I...er...I'm sorry. I don't remember my real name," I say quietly.

"Don't worry," says Debonaire. "Tarni's explained everything. Says she's calling you Magpie at the moment."

"Yes."

"Then that's good enough for me."

Debonaire looks like she is in her forties. Her wavy hair is dark and falls just below her shoulders. Her skin, brown. Her mouth is serious, but not at all thin. Her nose, ever so slightly hooked. She wears a green top with the arms cut off and a pair of cream shorts that show a pair of legs almost as muscled as her arms. Her feet are bare.

"I'll bet you're hungry," she says in a voice that echoes her physical appearance. "You've not eaten anything for quite a while."

"I...er..."

"I've got some steaks on the go. If you're up for it, come outside."

Outside it is too bright for my eyes and I have to cover them with my hand for a while.

"Sit in the shade," says Debonaire, pointing to a square plastic table with a great big umbrella on a pole sticking out of its middle. "Sit."

I pull out one of the white plastic chairs and sit down. The umbrella hides the sun away from me. Tarni – still clinging onto Dog – sits down too.

For the very first time I notice the smell. A beautiful, hot smoky sizzling sort of smell.

I twist in my seat to see Debonaire poking a long, brick barbecue with some tongs.

Dog wriggles in Tarni's arms, so she lowers him paw by paw to the ground. He scuttles off to lie at Debonaire's bare feet.

"Where's Candelabra?" I ask.

"He's there," says Tarni, indicating a large, buckled cage to one side of the silver caravan. "Stretching his wings a bit. Loads more room in there. Probably recover better in there."

In the cage I can see the bellbird perched on top of a long stick, a round mirror dangling down just in front of his beak. His head tilts from side to side before poking the mirror and making it swing.

I look at Tarni. She looks clean and refreshed. She grins at me.

"Imagine what would've happened if we'd collapsed kilometres from here? We'd be a dingo's dinner right now. All three of us."

"A *dingo's dinner*. That's what you said to me when you found me..." I try to think but fail to come up with a number, "...all those...days ago."

"True. Thankfully, we were nearby when you lost consciousness. Debonaire saw us and rescued us."

Two plastic beakers are dropped onto the table before us.

"Fizzy water," says Debonaire. "Wasn't me. Dog found you. I kept calling him, but he refused to come. I was going to give him an earful for being so disobedient. Make him spend the night outside. That was when I saw you both."

I look down at the tiny, furry dog with the big, sad eyes and the stubby, waggy little tail. He waddles next to me, craning his neck to peer up. So I lean over and half pat his head.

Debonaire goes back to the barbecue, and I take a sip of the iced fizzy water. I am so thirsty it almost burns the roof of my mouth.

I take a look around.

The silver caravan backs onto what appears to be a forest, so dense it is hard to see anything beyond the first couple of metres. I squeeze up my eyes but it is impossible.

The front of the caravan gleams in the sun and one side is covered in pretty pink climbing roses, twisting themselves through a trellis pinned to the caravan's frame.

Clothes billow on a makeshift washing line, my dress among them.

A squat wooden shed sits nearby, its door wide open. Inside I can just about make out a huge white refrigerator or freezer.

"How long did you say I was asleep?" I ask Tarni, who has finished all of her fizzy water.

"Two days. I think. Those peaches – or whatever they were – made us pretty sick, you know."

"Yes. And you're better now?"

"Right as an apple."

I nod. Then I lean in nearer to Tarni. "Have you told Debonaire about…you know?"

Tarni leans in too. "About what?"

"You know. About you and me."

"What're you on about?"

I sigh. "About…Professor Drongo and Madame Petrovsky?"

"Oh. Nah," she whispers. "Nah. I haven't." She glances at Debonaire putting the steaks on a plate. "I didn't think it was necessary."

"Good. That's probably best," I say. "Not until we're certain of things ourselves."

"Yes," says Tarni, not looking at me.

"Grub's up." Debonaire puts the large plate of steaks in the middle of the table, along with a big bowl of salad and some buttered slices of baguette. Tarni gets up and brings some smaller plates and some cutlery, spreading them out between all three of us. Finally, Debonaire fills up a jug with more fizzy water and blocks of ice from the freezer before sitting down in the chair opposite me.

"Well, it's good to have you back with us, Magpie," she says, holding up her plastic cup. "Here's to your very good health. Both of you."

I hold up my cup and Tarni holds up hers – even though it is empty – and we all tap the plastic together.

The steak almost evaporates on my tongue. And the salad is sweet and crunchy. The bread is soft and chewy, and I eat as much as my shrunken stomach will allow. Following it down with cup after cup of icy water.

"Thank you," I say. "That was…heavenly."

"My pleasure, kiddo," says Debonaire, winking. "Good to see young people with healthy appetites."

I look at Tarni's plate to see that there is not even a smudge of sauce or dressing left on it.

"Do you live here?" I ask as Debonaire fills my cup for the fourth time.

"Sure I do," she says, putting the jug back down on the table. "Wouldn't want to live anywhere else."

"It's…nice," I say, my eyes staring at the twisting roses.

"How long have you lived here?" asks Tarni.

Debonaire folds her arms and settles back in her chair.

"Let me think… Oh…well, let's just say, a long, long, time."

"Where were you before you came here?" I ask.

She smiles again. "Oh. Here. There. Everywhere. On land. In the air. At sea."

At sea. I think back to the pictures of submarines on the caravan wall.

"This is a long way from the sea," I say.

"Couldn't be further," agrees Debonaire.

"So what made you move out *here*?" I ask.

Debonaire sighs. "You're quite the stickybeak, aren't you, Magpie?" She looks around at her surroundings. "This is a tough land. Every day is a challenge. And I like challenges. Challenges keep you going. Challenges keep you...well...alive, I suppose. Real."

In my case, only just.

"And you live alone?"

"As alone as anyone can be, I suppose. I have Dog for company. I like things simple. Uncomplicated. Never had a telly or a radio. Don't care for them. Too much interference. But that's not to say I'm not delighted to have you here. You've made an interesting break to...well...everything."

Debonaire gets up and goes to her freezer shed, coming back with three cold-looking wrappers.

"Now, enough of these questions. Have a choccy ice," she says, handing them out.

Both Tarni and I waste no time in ripping off the wrappers and taking huge bites out of the ices. My first bite is far too big and confident and my teeth react in pain.

The same thing happens to Tarni. "Wery coal," she says, waving her hand up and down in front of her open mouth.

Debonaire grins and Dog looks up at us in hope.

I take a bath.

To one side of the caravan, Debonaire has an old ceramic bathtub set on some level concrete slabs. Nearby, a solid metal hand pump pulls water from a well below the ground.

Debonaire fits a rubber pipe over the end of the pump and puts the other end of the pipe into the tub.

"Great workout for the arms," she says as she starts moving the pump lever up and down. Clear, cold water spills out into the bath. The clearest, purest-looking water I have ever seen.

Debonaire pumps hard and, after a while, Tarni takes over, followed by me. It soon becomes clear why Debonaire has such muscular biceps. Pumping the water out is *impossibly* difficult work. As soon as Debonaire notices just how useless I am at it, she takes over again.

When the bath is reasonably full, Debonaire goes off with Dog to do some job or other, and I take off the T-shirt and climb into the bath. In the terrible heat of the middle of the afternoon the cold water feels amazing on my skin and I splash it all over my face.

Tarni sits nearby with her back to me.

"Why are you facing *that* way?" I ask.

"Well, I don't think it's right. You being *totally* naked. It's not respectful for me to see you. So I'll just keep my head in this direction, thank you very much."

I lie back in the bath and wash the water through my long hair. Debonaire has left a small shampoo bottle on the edge of the bath so I squeeze some out into my palm and rub it into my scalp. It smells familiar. In fact…it smells of someone I think I know… *My mother?*

I hold my hand under my nose, close my eyes tight, and try to imagine. Try to picture her. Try to see her hair and feel her hair and hear her voice.

But none of it ever quite comes.

And I feel as lost and confused and as angry as ever.

"My sister *was* here," says Tarni.

"What? Really?" Suddenly I am excited by this news – a distraction from my own frustrations – and some of the water splashes over the side of the tub. "Well?"

"Well what?"

"Where is she now?"

Tarni glances back.

"Well, she's not here. But…"

"But?"

"There's a letter."

"A letter? What does it say?"

"I haven't looked at it yet. In fact, I haven't even taken it from Debonaire yet."

I stop wringing my hair. "The sister you are chasing halfway across the country left you a letter and you haven't looked at it yet? Why not?"

"Because I wanted *you* to wake up. I wanted to make

sure *you* were okay first. And…well…we've come so far together, it's only right you hear her words too."

My heart stutters and even if my mother or father, or whoever it is that loves me, isn't here right now, I am so happy that Tarni is.

A dream?

Or a daydream, is it?

And another memory.

Glass. A huge expanse of glass before me. Like a wall.

Beyond the glass I can see the hills on the horizon and all the houses and roads and railway lines and rivers that lie in between.

A city. Busy and moving and colourful.

I can also see the sea, flickering with sunlight in the distance. Boats dotted across it.

I push my head up to the glass until my forehead rests cold against it.

I am far up. High. Soaring over this city in a crystal tower.

I make myself look down – my head squeaking against the glass – to see where the bottom of this palace begins.

Down below, right at the very foot of the tower, sits a long rectangular patch of playground. Brown, like it's made of soft, safe, bouncy cork. The markings of a basketball court neatly painted in white.

And on the playground...

Children. Lots of them.

Racing around. Throwing balls. Chasing each other. Laughing.

I suddenly feel younger than I am now. And I watch as they play their games and have their fun, and I want to join them.

But the thick glass is in the way. The distance between me and them is too much. There is no way I can get to them.

I bang on the glass but nobody can hear me.

I wave but nobody can see me.

I cry but nobody can console me.

This beautiful, glittering tower, I realize, feels like a prison.

Somehow, I shake myself back into the present and force myself out of the bath.

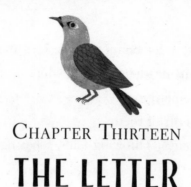

CHAPTER THIRTEEN
THE LETTER

Looking around Debonaire's plot of land, I realize that her coming here after spending time in submarines wasn't the strange move it first appears to be. After all, in a submarine, Debonaire would have been living in a long metal tube surrounded by billions of cubic litres of water. Now, with the caravan, she is living in a long metal tube surrounded by billions of cubic kilometres of *space*. No difference really. An isolated existence. Quiet. Alone.

Somehow completely right for her.

The compound itself, though, seems like a contradiction.

Inside the caravan, two rifles are hung on a wall like prize catches. But alongside them, a small painting of an English cottage with a thatched roof stakes its own claim to wall space.

By the sink, a clutter of oily wrenches and spanners and hammers and screwdrivers all pile up like a rugby scrum on one another, next to a delicate turquoise vase of purple flowers poised on a pretty coaster.

Outside, the cold, gleaming silver of the caravan looks at odds with the curling pink roses at one end. The broken-down truck – minus a curved strip of metal around its front wheel – shades the thriving tubs of tomatoes, green beans and pansies. The two dull, grey steel poles standing guard at either end of the washing line are joined by a loop of rope along which is pinned a colourful, twisting swirl of rainbow silk that spins in the breeze.

And it is the same with Debonaire herself.

She may be strong and tough, but she is also kind and gentle.

And definitely tactful.

"Here." Debonaire holds out the envelope to Tarni, her brown eyes reflecting the light raining in through the window. "I've got to go and water the pots. Come on, Dog." Dog jumps down from the soft seat onto the carpet. "Let's leave them to it."

They both go out through the door of the caravan, Dog's nose close to Debonaire's feet.

Tarni sits there with the envelope in her fingers like

she doesn't know what to do with it.

"Go on," I urge her. "Open it. You want to find out why your sister left, don't you?"

"Of course I want to find out," says Tarni.

"So why are you being so slow?"

She doesn't say anything.

"Come on! Hurry up!"

"But…" She looks very serious.

"What?"

"What if there's something in there that I don't want to find out about?"

"What do you mean?" I ask.

She thinks. "I don't really know what I mean. It's just that…now that I've come all this way, I'm worried what it might say."

I sit up straight. "Okay, then. Why don't you just throw away the letter?"

"What?"

"Throw it away. Scrunch it up –" I make a scrunching motion with my hands – "and just get rid of it."

Tarni looks horrified. "Don't be a galah," she says. "That'd be a ridiculous thing to do."

I smile at her. "Then open it."

Tarni shakes her head, sighs and then pushes her finger under the flap before ripping the envelope. She pulls out the piece of paper, stretches it open and starts to read.

"*Dear Atyeye*. That's what she called me. Atyeye. It means Little Sister. Sometimes I call her Yaye. Older Sister." Her eyes dart at me. "Yaye."

"Yes."

She continues. "*Dear Atyeye. I suppose if you're reading this it means you've done exactly what I imagined you would do. Which is...*" She struggles to read a word. "*...reassuring...as it proves I have known you very well indeed.*

"*Anyway,*" she says. "*As...flattering – and impressive – as it is that you've managed to follow me across this land, what I would like you to do now is turn round and go back home. Please, Atyeye, return to Utopia.*"

Tarni stops reading and looks over at me for some sort of reassurance. Unfortunately, there is nothing I can say. So, I say nothing.

Tarni carries on. "*Ma will need you. With me not around, Ma is going to need you more than ever. You need to be there for her. Help her through all of this. And go to school. Try and catch up all the work you've missed because of the times we spent in the bush. You should get a good education now that I won't be there to distract you.*

"*Don't worry about me. I will be okay. You know that.*

"And when everything is done and settled, and time has passed, I will see you again, Atyeye. But please don't count the days. They will be too long and there will be too many of them. Instead, remember your heritage, be good and live every day well.

"With love. For ever. B."

We sit there in silence for a long time, the sunlight bathing us in the caravan.

Suddenly, Tarni rips the piece of paper in half and throws it to the ground.

"What did you do that for?" I ask.

"You told me to do it, didn't you? I just wish I'd done it when you said. *Before* I read the miserable thing."

I really don't know what to say. "I don't know what to say," I say.

"You don't have to say anything," says Tarni, standing up and walking out of the caravan.

Outside, I find Tarni staring into the thick forest. Her arms are folded over her newly washed striped T-shirt and dungarees. Her face is like stone. Coming alongside her, I put my arm on her shoulder but she shakes it off.

"Pathetic little note. It doesn't say anything," Tarni grumbles. "What sort of stupid letter is it if it doesn't actually *tell* you anything? What's the point of it?"

"I don't know. It sounds like she doesn't want you

chasing after her all your life. Like she needs space to be herself. Like she wants *you* to be *yourself*."

"What, by helping Ma with the chores and going to school?" The words are spat out like bitter little bullets. "But she didn't care about school – she *never* cared about school." Tarni shakes her head. "No. It's not the stuff about going to school that I'm angry about. I'm angry because she hasn't explained anything to me. Me! Her best friend in the whole country! She's flown away from our life together, and now that I've caught her up, she's kept her teeth shut and flown away even further." I notice that her eyes look wet. "And that's not fair. I deserve more than that."

And with that, Tarni runs into the wood.

I stand waiting by the trees. Somewhere behind me I can hear Debonaire minding her own business by watering the tubs of vegetables and chatting to Dog.

A few minutes pass and I find myself feeling very stupid just standing there, waiting.

"Come out, Tarni," I call into the darkness of the forest. "Please. Just come out. It's no good sulking."

There is no answer.

"Tarni?"

Still no answer.

So, I follow her in.

Dark.

It is dark inside the wood. The trees are all so close together that there is little space between them for me to pass through. Their long, thick limbs twist into one another, overlapping and wrapping so tightly around themselves that they stop the sun reaching the ground.

It is almost like they are choking the life out of each other.

"Tarni," I whisper. Just being in this strange and dark place makes me feel like I need to whisper. "Where are you?"

I take a few steps into the wood, climbing over the looping roots of a grey gumtree. It gets darker.

"Tarni!"

I keep on, my bare, healing feet sometimes scratching on small spiky bushes.

Looking up I can see only the occasional speckle of light from the sky between the leaves.

"Where are you, Tarni? I'm coming to get you out of here."

I listen. There is no noise. No calls of animals. No squeaking of trees in the breeze. Not even the *sound* of a breeze. If Debonaire is talking to Dog nearby, I cannot hear her. There is nothing. Silence.

It is almost like I have wandered into a different world. Something unreal. Australia feels a million kilometres away. It is too cool. Too dark.

I start to feel a little scared.

"Tarni! Come on! Where are you?"

I take a few more steps. I have to hold my hands out in front of me to make sure that I don't knock into another tree or scratch into a wall of bramble. The more steps I take, the darker it gets. But I push on. I push on because Tarni does not belong in this dark place.

"Tarni? It's okay," I say. "I am here."

More steps.

Left then right…

And then I find her.

She is hard to see at first and I almost trip over her. But she is sitting right in front of me, her head in her hands.

"Hey! Tarni."

She rubs her eyes with her palms and looks up. It is obvious that she has been crying.

"Tarni," I say softly. "Come with me." I hold out my hand to her. "Come on."

She takes it.

We pick our way out of the dense forest, me in front with Tarni holding my hand just behind. She doesn't say anything. Neither do I. I just lead the way, and she follows.

It takes some time but eventually I can see the trees thinning again and the light starting to undo the bleakness of the wood. Pulling Tarni behind me, I step out into the overwhelming bright of day.

When my eyes adjust, I can see Debonaire standing before us, a glass in each hand. They look to me like glasses of rainbow.

"Sometimes," Debonaire starts, "it is necessary to go through a deep then deeper dark, and not to turn away." She smiles and leans towards us. "Lemonade, both?"

"Try this pair instead."

Debonaire is pulling some old boots out of a large box. The first two pairs I have tried on have been a little too big, so she hands me a different pair – a pair of solid, purple ankle-high walking boots with fraying laces that go on for ever.

"When your sister passed through here, she was in good spirits," Debonaire says, tugging the laces through some of the holes on one of the boots. "In fact, she was in much better shape than either of you, I have to say. I think she'd managed to avoid the poisonous fruit a little more successfully." She drops the boot on the ground in front of me and I start feeding my foot into it.

"Did she tell you anything?" Tarni asks eagerly, the lemonade in her glass long gone. "About what had happened?"

Debonaire pulls another pair of boots out of the box and inspects them in the light. "We talked," she says. "Wise girl, your sister. Strong-minded. Capable."

Tarni spends the next few quiet minutes looking confused, while I pull on the second boot and tighten up the laces before walking in a very small circle.

"These feel good," I say, bouncing up and down in the boots. "They fit much better."

"You don't want to try these ones?" Debonaire waves the other boots in the air.

"No. Thank you. These fit perfectly. Are you sure I can have them?"

"It's better that they keep your feet healthy and free from blisters, than having to sit in a box for the rest of human existence," she says.

"Did she tell you where she was going?" Tarni bursts out. "When she left here. Did she tell you where she was going?"

"Um...yes. She did," replies Debonaire. "She said she was going to go to Karlu Karlu." Debonaire stares at Tarni, and Tarni stares right back.

"Where's that?" I ask.

Debonaire points with a boot in a rough direction just past the caravan. "It's about eighty or ninety clicks north-westerly. It's a collection of massive rocks, many of which are stacked on top of each other. Some people refer to it as the Giant's Marbles. It's a sacred site. Tourist site too, nowadays. Hotel nearby. Just off the Stuart Highway."

Debonaire pushes the boots back into the box. "Did your sister say anything about it in the letter she wrote you?"

Tarni's eyes skip over to me.

"Um…no," she says. But then her eyes look away, down to the ground. "No. She didn't say *why* she was going there. But she did say that I was to go on and follow her."

I open my mouth to say something but Tarni's head snaps up and she stares hard at me, warning me to be quiet. So, I close my mouth.

"She said that I have to go to Karlu Karlu. She said I would find her there."

"Right." Debonaire says nothing else but picks up the box and carries it to the shed from which she dragged it.

"What are you doing?" I whisper. "Brindabel didn't say that. She said you should go back—"

"Sssh," says Tarni. "It doesn't matter what the letter said. I'm going there. *You* don't have to. *You* can go back to your posh city house if you want." *Posh city house?* My mind jumps back to the sad, lonely glass tower. "But *I'm* walking all the way to Karlu Karlu. And no one's going to stop me."

"But if Brindabel wanted you to go to Karlu Karlu she would have said."

"Don't care," says Tarni like a petulant toddler. "I'm going. If Yaye was still here, I wouldn't be in all this mess."

"Mess?" I ask.

Tarni looks at me like I've said something ridiculous. "I *have* just killed somebody, y'know?"

"We both have," I reply.

"Oh, you've not killed anyone," she dismisses. "Even though you believe so."

"How can you be so sure?"

She turns away from me and starts walking off.

"I just know."

"NO, YOU DON'T," I shout. "You don't know *anything*!"

CHAPTER FOURTEEN

THE MUSIC

We help Debonaire with the supper. Tarni slices lettuce and tomatoes for the fresh salad, while I top and tail long, thin green beans. Debonaire cleans up some new potatoes and fires up the barbecue ready for some of her home-made sausages. Dog hangs around sniffing the air and getting under everybody's feet.

"So, Magpie," Debonaire asks. "What do you think brought you here? Can you remember?"

I scoop up the dead heads of the beans and drop them into a rubbish bowl. "I don't know," I say.

"She says that a lot," Tarni laughs. "It's the thing I've probably heard her say most since I found her."

Debonaire doesn't respond. "What *can* you remember about your life?"

I measure everything that I *could* say alongside

everything that I *should* say. And then I say what I can.

"I remember a cat called Violet Crumbles. I remember a tiled floor covered in squares and diamonds. I remember an old woman. I have a memory of birds flying past me and a tall glass tower. That's about it."

I don't mention that I also remember that I can be a spoilt brat. Nasty and sarcastic. I keep those bits hidden.

"She remembers winning a marble off someone with a stupid name, too," says Tarni. "And some pointless poetry."

Debonaire tsks. "That's not much. So you can't remember your parents? Or even where you live? You can't remember your name?"

I shake my head. "No. I can't remember any of it."

Tarni suddenly gets up from the table and takes the full salad bowl to where Debonaire is standing. When she comes back, she stares down at Dog.

"That's sad," says Debonaire. "It's not a very nice feeling – not knowing who you are or where you belong. Everyone needs to feel comfortable with their own identity. If you don't even know what that identity is... well...it's very difficult."

For some reason, I feel like crying.

But I don't. Because before I can start, Debonaire asks another question.

"Any idea how long you've played the violin?"

I snort. "I can't play the violin," I say.

"You sure?" says Debonaire. "You're walking around the Australian Outback with one in your hands. You haven't just abandoned it yet and left it for the camels to kick about. It must be important to you."

My eyes drift over to Tarni, but she is still staring down at Dog.

"No. I'm sure I can't play it."

"Have you tried?"

"What?"

Debonaire wipes her hands on a cloth and comes over to the plastic table. "I said, have you tried playing it?"

"Er…no. I haven't."

"Why not?"

I think hard. "I was going to…but…" I remember Tarni rushing me off to find food after the hungry night in the cave. Then I remember the incident with the Drongos where I found out the true value of the violin. *Three million dollars!* And where I found out that I had stolen it. Since then, with all the worry, I hadn't even thought about taking the violin out of its case.

Debonaire drops the handcloth on the table and goes into the caravan. A few seconds later she comes back out holding the violin case.

"Here," she says, laying the case on the table. She pops open the locks at either end without putting in the codes and opens up the lid. Inside sits the violin. "Play."

"What?" I smile.

"Take it out and play."

I grin over at Tarni but she is *still* staring at Dog.

"But…I…" I stutter.

"Magpie." Debonaire's voice is serious and strong. "Play."

I sit there for a few seconds unsure of what to do. Then I reach out to remove the bow from its holder. The moment I turn the lock holding the bow in place, something weird happens.

Something clicks.

In my mind.

I take the bow and twist the end screw, tightening the bow hair. Once it is tight enough, I automatically reach into a tiny compartment of the case and pull out a small, round plastic pot of rosin.

Rosin, I think to myself. *This is rosin. I know this is rosin!*

I pop off the top of the rosin and take it out. It is a clear golden colour with a strip of cloth attached to one end. Picking it up by the cloth I begin to rub the rosin along the length of the bow. Up and down. Up and down.

Until I am certain that there is enough of the chalky substance on it.

Then I lay the bow down carefully on the table before unstrapping the Velcro holding the violin.

I look up at Debonaire, who is staring at me, smiling. I can also see Tarni watching me out of the corner of her eye. Suspicious almost.

I lift the violin out before opening another compartment in the metal case. Inside sits the shoulder rest – a curved strip of metal covered in rubber with two adjustable feet at either end. I turn the feet so they are facing the right way and then push the whole shoulder rest onto the wide end of the violin until it is locked into position. It all feels so natural to me, like my hands are doing it all on their own.

Standing up, I hook the violin between my chin and my shoulder. I take up the bow, balancing it perfectly between my thumb and forefinger.

I feel the strings beneath my fingers.

I take a deep breath.

Suddenly, in my head, I can hear a tune. Orchestral. Gentle. Melodic. It eases itself in with strings, I think. And flutes and clarinets join in.

I realize that I have heard it playing in my head before – walking across this red land with Tarni some days ago.

I hear the strings build, then one of the clarinets raises its head.

But the strings compete harder.

They fight to get louder and louder.

And then, when it sounds like there is going to be an orchestral explosion…

I start to play.

Sad. Slow. My fingers dance across the fingerboard, stretching across the strings. I pull the bow over them as I make the notes sing out.

I keep my eyes closed. I am not here. I am somewhere else.

The music becomes prettier. Lighter. More spritely. Making my fingers reach further along the neck. Occasionally there is a flourish. A quick flutter of notes like a bird soaring into the sky. Like Candelabra flying up into the blue. My fingers dance, I hold my breath. The melody swoops and stirs and I feel myself swaying with the music.

My music.

The music I am playing.

As I play, I sense the orchestra – the strings, the woodwind, the horns, the percussion. I hear the violins following my lead. I hear the plucking of the double basses. I hear the flutes twittering. The oboes, the clarinets, the bassoons. I hear it all accompanying me.

The boots on my feet are not standing on the red dust. They are standing on the wooden slatted boards of a concert hall somewhere. A vast auditorium before me. The audience watching.

The staccato strings pulse beneath the ringing tones, and I feel a slight brushing against my cheek as I realize that one of the hairs on the bow has broken. But I ignore it. I play on regardless, the hardened tips of my fingers – *Ah, yes! That is why they are hard* – securely pinpointing each and every note.

At one point the music almost accelerates, and my hand races up and down the neck, and my bowing becomes feverish.

On I play. On and on. Automatically. Lost in a different world.

Until, eventually, I slow and take the last few strokes of the bow to the end of my part.

I open my eyes to see Debonaire and Tarni both staring at me.

"Wow," says Debonaire, grinning.

"Deadly," says Tarni. "Totally deadly." She seems sad.

I lower the violin from my shoulder.

"Tchaikovsky's Violin Concerto in D major," I say. "Opus thirty-five. First movement. I can play the second and third movements too. If you'd like."

"It is called the *Karpilowsky*," I say, holding the violin up to the light. "The *Karpilowsky Stradivarius*. All Stradivarius violins have a name, and this one is the *Karpilowsky*."

"And you thought kwementyaye was a difficult name to say," says Tarni.

"It's a nickname, really," I continue. "Named after the violinist Daniel Karpilowsky, who once owned it. Karpilowsky lived in Hollywood and played on many famous records and film scores of the 1940s and 1950s. Then the violin passed on to Harry Solloway – another Hollywood musician. Unfortunately, the violin was stolen from Solloway's house in Los Angeles in 1953 and disappeared for nearly seventy years. It was only recently rediscovered. The person who owns it now…well… I assume they loan it to me. To play."

"See," says Tarni, still not properly looking at me. "I said you hadn't stolen it. I said you weren't a thief."

"Impressive," says Debonaire over her shoulder as she turns the sausages on the barbecue. "But has any of this triggered your memory? Do you know who you are now?"

I put the violin back into the titanium temperature-controlled case and think. I struggle, almost straining the blood vessels in my head. Then I relax and try to let it come naturally. Gently. *Surely I must know now!*

231

But…

"No," I say. "I still don't know my name."

"Would be easy enough to find *that* out," says Debonaire. "Prodigy like yourself." Some fat spurts out of a sausage and a whole column of smoke billows up into Debonaire's face. She waves it away. "Is there anything else you can remember? You know a lot about the violin and its previous owners. There must be other stuff you can remember now."

I think hard again.

"The diamond floor. The tiles," I say. "I think it is the floor in the foyer of some concert hall I have played in."

"Good," says Debonaire. Tarni seems to be staying very quiet. "Anything else?"

"Madame Petrovsky," I close my eyes to try and keep my mind focused. "Madame Petrovsky is my teacher. She is my violin tutor."

"I don't know," mumbles Tarni. "Tchaikovsky. Karpilowsky. Petrovsky. There seem to be a lot of -*sky* names filling my brain today." She is trying hard to force the joke.

A flash of memories passes across my retinas. Memories of Madame Petrovsky's face. Pale. Stern. Unsmiling. A finger wagging, keeping time.

You play with no heart, I hear her say. *You have no*

feeling when you play. Imagine Violet Crumbles dying in the triste *section. Play like she is dying. Play with sadness and love in the tips of your fingers.*

Then a memory of me sitting in the back of a long car with Madame Petrovsky, her finger pointing to the sky outside.

Look how blue the sky is, little one, she says. Look how blue and beautiful. If only there was music as magnificent and as graceful and as perfect as the sky. Now that would be a symphony or concerto worth hearing.

Then another final memory. The one I had before.

Madame Petrovsky waving at me across the foyer of the concert hall.

Come on, she calls. Quickly. You are going to be late.

She is holding the door open for me and I pass through, the violin case strapped over my back.

"What about your parents?" Debonaire asks, spearing sausages onto a large plate with a long fork. "Can you remember them? You *must* be able to remember them now!"

My mind struggles again. "No."

"Can you picture their faces?"

"No. I can't see them. I don't know why. I just can't make them out in my mind. But…" I squeeze my eyes together as tight as I possibly can. And I sniff. "I'm sure

233

I can smell my mother's perfume." I smile. "I think…it is all *slowly…very* slowly…coming back to me."

That evening, after we have all demolished Debonaire's big haystack pile of home-made sausages – with Tarni feeding Dog a couple surreptitiously under the plastic table – I open up the violin case and play some more.

Some of the pieces I can remember the names of. Some of them I can't.

"You know," says Debonaire, clapping me at the end of a piece, "I don't think Magpie is quite the right name for you."

"No?" I ask.

"No. It's not. I think from now on we should call you… Maestro. *Master of music.*"

"Maestro." Tarni smiles. "Yes."

As the sun sets behind us, I am standing centre stage in the deep red desert with my audience of two (and a dog and a bellbird), eyes closed, playing myself back into existence. Slowly – and at last – I am beginning to understand a little of who I actually am.

Chapter Fifteen
THE ANGENTE

The following morning I wake up and, kneeling on the bed next to a still sleeping Tarni, I take a look at the photographs of ships and submarines and all their crews that Debonaire has pinned onto the wall.

The ships are big and grey and impressive. The submarines are black and sleek and half underwater. HMAS *Selaphiel* reads the name on one. The crews are smart and neatly lined up. I squint my eyes to try and spot Debonaire, but I struggle to pick her out from the crowd.

So I change out of my Elvis T-shirt nightgown back into my mended black dress – it might not be suitable for this terrain, but at least I know it's *mine* – pull on the thin socks and tough purple boots that Debonaire has given to me, and open the door onto the far-too-bright day.

"Good morning, Maestro," says Debonaire, packing away the hammock on which she is sleeping while the two strange girls she rescued borrow her bed. "It's yet another beautiful day."

"It is," I say.

"You hungry? I've got a whole tonne of waffles and syrup if you fancy them. And some packs of bacon. And eggs."

I help her pull the ropes from the hammock down off the trees.

"Where do you get all this food from?" I ask. "There are no shops around here."

"Well, mostly it's possible to live off the land but –" she taps the side of her nose – "heh! I have my methods." Debonaire feeds the folded hammock into a cloth storage bag.

"You've got a car?" I ask.

"Mmm. Unfortunately, at the moment, old Engelbert's not going anywhere."

"Engelbert?"

Debonaire points over to the broken-down truck sitting next to the tubs of tomatoes, green beans and pansies.

"Engelbert. I still need to weld on his wheel arch – it dropped off. And his distributor's blown. Got to replace it."

Debonaire takes the newly bagged hammock and hangs it over a hook on the inside of the shed.

"If you want to wait around a while, I could take you over to Tennant Creek. See if we can get you back to your folks. They must be going nuts."

They must be, I think.

But then I think back to the memory of me high in the sky in a shiny glass tower. And I remember the terrible sense of loneliness – the feeling of being trapped in a prison.

I think back to the memories – if that's what they are – of the bitter, spiteful girl that I obviously must be in the real world.

Then I think of Tarni and her sister. Happy in this wide-open landscape.

Together.

"You know…I was hoping that you'd travel with *me*," comes a voice from behind.

I turn to see Tarni hanging out of the doorway, her hair all mussed up from a poor night's sleep.

"To Karlu Karlu. I was hoping that you'd help me get there."

I look back at Debonaire.

"Maestro?" she asks.

I smile. And I nod. "I suppose Karlu Karlu seems like

as good a place as any to be rescued from."

Debonaire nods. "I thought you might say that. Good call."

"Yeah!" Tarni jumps out of the doorway and punches the air.

"I've sketched you out a map." Debonaire hands Tarni a strange piece of A4 paper folded in half. "Major landmarks to look out for. Generally, as a rule, keep the Iytwelepenty mountains on your right-hand side. Don't go over them, just use them to guide you. Follow them and they will lead you to Karlu Karlu."

Tarni opens up the paper for a second or two before folding it back in half and slipping it into the front pocket on her dungarees. "Thank you," she says. "I am moving out of my people's country now, so I don't know the songs to guide me."

"Then *create* a song," says Debonaire.

"What?"

"Create one. Make a new song." Debonaire points at me. "You've got a world-class violinist to help you, so make one."

Tarni looks stunned. "But…that's not what we do. We follow the songs of our ancestors—"

"So *become* an ancestor," interrupts Debonaire, combing her hand through her thick, dark hair. "Create a song so that hundreds of years from now, *your* descendants will sing it to travel over this land."

"I...I don't know," says Tarni.

"You're beginning to sound like *me*," I say, holding my violin in its case in the air.

Tarni looks me up and down and then begins to nod. "Yeah. Okay. You're right. We'll make a new song. That will be good."

"You know he's probably well enough to be set free now, don't you?"

We are all standing in front of the spacious cage that Candelabra has been enjoying himself in over the last few days.

Debonaire opens the little door and grabs hold of Candelabra, pulling him out.

"His wing is pretty much fixed. See?" She stretches the wing for Tarni to see. "I'm sure he'd be capable of flying back to his home."

Tarni says nothing.

"Perhaps you should let him go now." Debonaire looks at Tarni.

"No," Tarni replies. "Not yet."

"Why not?"

"I think he still needs a bit more time. I don't think he's completely recovered yet."

"But—"

"No." Tarni sounds very definite. "No. Not yet. He's coming with me."

Debonaire smiles and nods. "Okay. I understand. Wings are tricky things to heal."

Debonaire hands me a small rucksack that she has filled with some of her home-made treats and a couple of extra bottles of fresh water.

"Should keep you going for a while," she says as Tarni and I prepare to set off. "I've even included one of my specialities." She has a proud look on her face. "Wattleseed bread."

"Oh no!" Tarni and I say at the same time.

"What?" asks Debonaire.

"We've had a lot of experience with wattleseed bread," I say.

"Yeah," agrees Tarni. "A lot."

Debonaire shakes her head and doesn't ask any more. When we are ready, all three of us (and Dog) walk towards the north, tacking round the edge of the long, dark wood. Me with Debonaire's rucksack on my back, a pandanus-leaf hat on my head and the violin case at my side. Tarni with her big canvas bag over her shoulder and Candelabra back in his makeshift cage.

"We'll take you over the hill, then Dog and I will leave you to it," says Debonaire. "Last thing you need is an ancient being like me wrinkling your style."

"Thank you, Debonaire," I say. "For everything."

"No probs, kiddo," she says. "It's been my pleasure. But be careful. This is still a tough land."

I suddenly remember what she said when first I met her. "A *tough land, where every day is a challenge.*"

Debonaire smiles. "But challenges are good things. Challenges and tests. Without them, we might as well spend the rest of our time in bed." Debonaire looks at me and then she looks at Tarni. "And we *all* have tests that we need to pass – every single one of us. And sometimes – if we're lucky – we pass them without even knowing."

Suddenly Dog gives a little bark, so I bend over and happily pat him on the head.

Once we are over the hill, we all stop walking.

Nobody says a word.

I look up at Debonaire. Her face is serious and strong. Her eyes dark but bright. I lean in and hug her, feeling her arms close around me, squeezing tightly. Her biceps are hard against my back, but she smells of soft, fresh lemons.

After a while we release each other and she gives me the warmest smile ever before turning to Tarni.

The two of them stand respectfully in front of one another. Nothing is said between them, just a nod of acknowledgement from one to the other and back again. It reminds me of the way Tarni and Eddy said goodbye all those days (or is it weeks?) ago.

Then, without any more fuss, Debonaire turns and walks away from us. Dog skitters between our feet for a few seconds before rushing off to catch up with his mistress.

We stand there, watching in silence as they both make their way over the red dust up towards the top of the hill.

We walk for the time it takes the sun to arc itself further into the sky. Neither of us really saying anything. At the top of a small mountain, we stop and turn round to look back at the land.

In the distance we can pick out the wide wood, which

sits next to Debonaire's silver caravan. We both squint hard, trying to focus.

But it is strange.

Where I would expect to see the silver caravan, there is nothing. I look at Tarni and I can tell that she is thinking the same thing.

We stand there for a few minutes, struggling to see it.

At last, Tarni speaks.

"Angente," she whispers to herself.

"What does that mean?" I ask.

"Angente. It means *mirage*," says Tarni.

I nod and, without saying anything else, we both turn to continue towards Karlu Karlu.

PART THREE

Symphony – An elaborate musical composition
for full orchestra.

(Oxford English Dictionary)

CHAPTER SIXTEEN

THE TERRIBLE SMELL OF SMOKE

Time passes as the land flattens out ahead of us and the aywerte thins.

"What's this?" I ask as we are about to step out onto an empty, open area. As soon as I set foot on it, it becomes obvious.

"It's another road," says Tarni.

The scruffy, half-abandoned highway looks as if it has seen no tyre for a very long time. Weeds crack through the tarmac, pushing their way from the dirt beneath to the brutal glare of light above. Small tufts of grass nibble away at the edges of the road, trying to meet one another in the centre. Even the tarmac itself looks grey and dusty, like some long-forgotten thing in an old person's cupboard.

Which is all ironic because a car is coming along it. Towards us.

Right now.

Lightning thoughts fly through both of our minds.

"Is that…?" starts Tarni. But she doesn't finish. There is no need. Because we both recognize the white Jeep lumbering roughly from left to right.

"Mrs Drongo! Run!" I shout as we both skip over to the other side of the road and begin racing off towards the horizon. Candelabra is being shaken in his cage and making his alarm-bell noise louder than ever. The rucksack on my back bounces up and down hard against me, thumping me. The violin case knocks repeatedly into my legs.

I look over my shoulder to see the Jeep turn off the road into the dirt – red dust kicking up into the air – only a few hundred metres behind us.

"She's seen us!" I call to Tarni, who doesn't say anything.

We sprint off over a small ridge, only to find right in front of us, for as far as I can see…

A salt pan.

Tarni makes a little yelp under her out-of-breath breathing. Then she points. "Straight across it! Run straight across it!"

So, we tear down the other side of the ridge and race over the cracked dry salt pan.

"But…we're out…in the open!" I shout as my feet thump over the white crust. "If she wants…to shoot us…"

"Let's…just…hope…" Tarni says, over Candelabra's continual yawping, "…she…doesn't."

"Yes!" I call.

Tarni nods before turning to look straight ahead again.

We are almost in the middle of the salt pan, when there is a huge roar as the Jeep bounces over the ridge and down the other side.

"She's coming!" I squeak.

"Good!" says Tarni, her sandals slapping against the salt.

I don't look behind any more. I keep on running. The violin case is knocking a dirty bruise onto my leg and sweat is streaking off my brow. But I am thankful for Debonaire's old boots, which make running across the desert much easier than with a shoe and a slipper!

There seems to be more light in my eyes than normal and I suddenly realize that the pandanus hat on my head has disappeared. It must have come off in the first few seconds of running.

The end of the salt pan is in sight. I can see the place where it turns back into red dust and green spikes.

"Keep going," says Tarni. "Nearly there."

"Is she still coming?" I call back to her.

"I hope so."

"What do you mean?"

It is at that point that the sound of the Jeep's engine changes behind us. Instead of the continual low rattling roar, there is a high-pitched whine followed by another. Then another. There is also a splatter sound that comes straight after.

I hear Tarni stop running, so I stop too.

I turn round to look and I can see that, far off across the salt pan, the Jeep is tilted at a funny angle. It is as though one of the front wheels has disappeared completely.

"Yes!" says Tarni.

I peer to see more clearly through the heat haze. The wheel hasn't disappeared. It has sunk under the salt crust into the mud below. The engine squeals and black dirt sprays into the air behind the Jeep. Suddenly, the whole truck shifts as the other front wheel slumps into the wet mud.

"Deadly!" shouts Tarni. "You can't drive heavy trucks over the salt pans. They always get stuck. You'd think she might know that. Come on, let's get out of here."

I say nothing, but sprint with Tarni off across the salt plain and out into the desert.

In the evening, before the darkness crashes in, we make a start on the new song.

Tarni has memorized a number of different points along our journey. A fallen down tree. An outcrop of red rock. A dip in the land. A clump of thick kungaberry bushes.

She begins to put the Alyawarre words for such things together. Then she sings, trying to make the words scan.

"A-*yer-rer-re-arl-ket-yer-re-ath-et-he-ke-ath-irt-ne-kwe-ne-ar-ne*," she sings with virtually no melody. "*Ayer-rerre-arlket-yerre-athet-heke-athirt-nekwe-near-ne*."

I listen as she works out a rhythm for singing the words. Sometimes she drops in a few more syllables to make the rhythms work. Then, when I feel she is settling upon something, I play.

I play a few basic notes. I try them out as she sings. Once or twice Tarni wrinkles up her nose, so I take the music down a different route. I use a different key.

Tarni has to adjust her voice a little to follow my key. This happens a few times until—

Something magical happens.

I try F sharp minor.

Everything slides into place. I come up with a melody that weaves itself around the words that Tarni is singing.

Tarni smiles at me as she sings and I smile back at her as I play. Each of us an extension of the other, overlapping perfectly. Like pennies stacked on top of one another.

It is a wonderful, wonderful moment.

Sitting there cross-legged in the middle of the desert, a fire glimmering warmly in front of us, Tarni and I make music into the fading light of day.

I am strapped in to my seat.

I look around me. There are very few seats. Eight or ten at the most. It all seems so small. On the seat right next to me is the violin case – the belt wrapped round it. I feel like I want to laugh – a violin with its own aeroplane seat! But for some reason I stop myself.

This does not feel like a time for laughing.

I turn my head to the window and stare down. The land below the occasional wisp of cloud looks orange. The afternoon sun glares down at it and the ground looks scarred and burnt.

Across the aisle is the only other passenger as far as I can tell. She sits there asleep, her head lolling on one side.

Madame Petrovsky.

Suddenly, hundreds and hundreds of birds – *bellbirds,*

are they? – thick like a fog – race past, darkening my tiny window and the plane starts shaking. Then there is a bang.

I grip my armrests.

Madame Petrovsky wakes up and looks over at me, confused.

The plane begins to shake even more violently. A rattling noise fills the air. Out of the window, I look back to see that there is something not quite right with the wing. There is something missing.

A red light above the door to the cockpit comes on. A high-pitched, anxious voice over the intercom says something but I cannot make it out.

There is a terrible smell of smoke.

And then I can sense the plane curving downwards. The violin leans forward against its belt. I grip even harder onto the arms of the seat as the engine roars.

Outside the horizon is quickly becoming vertical in the glass of the window.

Suddenly I feel Madame Petrovsky in front of me. Her arms are holding onto my shoulders, squeezing them. She pulls herself closer into me, covering me. I cannot see anything.

It is like she is shielding me. Protecting me.

Everything is happening so quickly.

I lift my hands from the armrests and put them round

Madame Petrovsky. I can feel her starting to drop away from me as the plane turns. So I clutch at her silk dress and pull her near as my feet lift away from the floor and the shoe on my left foot slips off.

Madame Petrovsky's head is next to mine. She says something into my ear.

"Close your eyes, detenysh," she says. "Close your eyes and be brave."

I try to tug her nearer to me. I am so scared.

But I do not close my eyes.

And I wish I had.

Because the last thing I see is the face of Madame Petrovsky as she falls away from me towards the front of the plane. It is an image that I have seen too many times recently.

Madame Petrovsky screaming.

And then…

Silence.

Blackness.

Nothing.

I sit up.

My whole body is wet with sweat and my heart feels as though it is wired up to the grid.

It is dark, but the fading embers of fire are throwing a glow over our camping place. I reach out next to me to feel Tarni sleeping, but she is not there.

"Tarni?" I whisper.

"You were having one of your dreams," she says, and I can see her sitting on the other side of the fire. "You were jumping about and making a load of noise, so I came over here to try and get some kip without your elbows banging into me."

"I know what happened to me," I say, ignoring her. "There...there was a plane crash. I was involved in a plane crash. That's why I was lost in the desert. I managed to survive. But...oh no...Madame Petrovsky...she died. And the pilot. They both died. I think." I feel terrible. I feel like I want to be sick. "They're dead."

I see Tarni nodding on the other side of the dying flames.

"Madame Petrovsky...she tried to protect me. She... she...she held on to me. I think she saved my life."

I feel tears in my eyes.

"She called me detenysh. That was her name for me. That's what she would call me. Detenysh. It's Russian for *little one*."

Tarni doesn't say anything. She sits there staring at me for a while.

"They're both dead," I say, feeling the tears tracking down my cheeks. "They're both dead."

"They might not be," says Tarni, but there is such a lack of force in the statement that it sounds like she is simply saying the words and not meaning them. "They... might not be dead."

I look over at her and I can tell from her eyes that she knows what she says isn't the truth.

"No," I say. "They're dead."

I wipe the wetness from my cheeks and we sit there saying nothing for a long time.

CHAPTER SEVENTEEN

THE STOLEN

"My ipmenhe…my grandmother. She never knew her own ma. Not properly, anyway."

We are walking. As we walk, Tarni talks.

"She was taken, you see. When she was a kid."

I turn to look at Tarni. "What do you mean, *taken*?"

"She was one of the Stolen Generations."

"What?"

She stops and stares at me. "There's so much stuff you don't know, isn't there?"

"It's getting less each day," I joke.

Tarni ignores me and starts walking again.

"The Stolen Generations were First Country kids taken away from their parents by the government."

"What? Why?"

"The government thought it was the best thing for

them. They thought that it was better to split up families than to have children growing up respecting their traditional culture.

"My grandmother was taken one day when she was about two. That's what Ma tells me, anyway. She was taken to an institution where she was taught to be less First Country. They would teach her European history and how to speak English. They taught the boys how to be strong to work in the fields and in factories, and the girls how to be good house servants.

"If you behaved badly, the women who ran the place – religious women – would beat you and make you go all day without tucker."

I shake my head. "Really? That's horrible."

"Yeah. I know. Thousands of kids were taken. Men from the government would roll up at the outstations in their cars and just take them."

"Couldn't their parents get them back?"

"Nah. There was nothing they could do. It was the law, see. The government had decided that was what was going to happen, so that's what happened. Thousands of kids grew up not knowing who they really were. My grandmother never even knew her real name. She spent her whole life stuck with the name the religious women gave her."

"What was that?"

"Evangeline."

"Pretty name," I say.

"A pretty name but not her real name."

We step around a thick clump of buffalo grass.

"What happened to your grandmother?" I ask.

"When she was fourteen she ran away from the institution – the mission. She'd had enough so she got out. Climbed out of a window one night and cleared off."

"Good."

"Went back to the country she knew she'd been taken from. But she never found her ma. Then later she met my atyemeye – my grandfather – and had my ma and four other kids. So she was okay in the end. Had a real good life, I think.

"But loads of the Stolen Generations *weren't* okay. Loads of them were really messed up." Tarni tugs her canvas bag tighter over her shoulder. "Just because the government thought they were better than the First Country people and wanted us to disappear."

"That's evil," I say.

"Yeah," says Tarni. "It *is* evil."

It is during our lunch break that everything goes wrong.

We are eating some of Debonaire's sweet potato pies when I notice Tarni staring at me.

"What?" I ask with a mouthful of pastry.

"What?" she asks back.

"What are you staring at me for?"

"I'm not staring." She spits a tiny orange speck into the space between us.

"You are," I say. "You've been doing that a lot recently. Staring at me and looking like you are trying to avoid saying something."

"I'm not," she says, but there is a flicker of something across her face.

"You're lying," I snap. "You're not telling the truth."

Tarni wipes the crumbs from her hands and stands up.

"This is nuts," she says. "We need to get going. Come on."

"No," I say, also standing up. "We're not going anywhere. Please. Not until you've told me whatever it is you're not telling me."

Tarni tugs at one of her crocodile earrings. "You're talking jibber again. You're not making sense."

"Tarni!" I shout and my voice echoes off the nearby hills.

Candelabra starts his high-pitched bell-rattling noise again.

"Look what you've done now," says Tarni. "You've set him off." She begins to move away.

"I don't care!" I reach out and grab her by the shoulder.

"Don't you DARE touch me!" Tarni says, shaking my hand off her. "Do that again and I'll lay you out flat!"

"Then tell me why you keep looking at me that way! You've been doing it for ages."

She turns and carries on walking.

So I grab her arm again.

Suddenly, Tarni twists and pushes me hard in the chest, sending me falling backwards. I stumble but manage to keep myself upright.

"TELL ME!" I scream. I feel all the anger and frustration that has been inside me for so long burst out through the surface and into the air around me. "TELL ME!"

Tarni stares with bitterness at me. She drops the canvas bag to the ground and then lowers Candelabra's cage. She looks like she is preparing to fight me.

"Okay," she says like a snake spitting venom. "Okay. You want me to tell you why I keep looking at you, yeah? Well, I'll do better than that." She does a sort of swagger. "In fact, I'll do *much* better than that.

"I'll tell you your name."

"What?"

"You wanna know your name, don't you? You wanna know who you really are? Well, I'm going to tell you!"

I feel confused. "What are you saying? I don't understand."

"Well, *I* do. I know your name. I can't forget it. For days it's been spinning round inside my nut. Round and round it goes. Keeping me awake."

"I don't believe you."

Tarni doesn't respond. Instead she points a finger at me. "You're *not* Maestro. You're *not* Magpie. You're not even Moonflower." She moves like she's planting her feet solidly into the ground. "You're Sienna Marie Silke Martha Vanderbolt."

Sienna Marie Silke Martha Vanderbolt.

BANG.

Everything comes.

Everything comes back like an ocean wave.

"*Sienna Marie Silke Martha Vanderbolt*," Tarni says again, almost relishing every single syllable. "*The thirteen-year-old violin-playing daughter of multi-millionaire celebrity lawyer Roy Vanderbolt and his wife, Delphine.*"

It is like all the air inside my lungs has been sucked out. Or someone has kicked me hard in the stomach. Or both.

Tarni keeps on. "*Travelling to Darwin to perform with*

the Darwin Philharmonic Orchestra, Tchaikovsky's Violin Concerto in D major." She raises her eyebrows. "Flying in her father's private plane with her Russian violin tutor, Anastasia Petrovsky. Unfortunately, the plane encountered difficulties and crashed in the Northern Territory, two hundred kilometres north of Alice Springs. Rescuers recovered the remains of Ms Petrovsky and also those of the pilot. However, there was no sign of Ms Vanderbolt. It is believed that she survived the crash and is lost somewhere in the outback. Police are in a race against time to find the missing girl in the infamous Australian bush, which can claim the lives of the lost in as little as forty-eight hours."

I stand there. Not moving. Stun-gunned with all this information.

"Is that enough?" asks Tarni. "Does that fill in all the gaps?"

"How do you know all this?"

Tarni bends over and pulls something out of her canvas bag. "The gas station," she says. "I found out at the gas station." She throws something towards me and I instinctively catch it.

It is a newspaper.

I look at it and see that on the front cover is a photograph of the girl I have seen in Tarni's mirror.

Me.

SEARCH CONTINUES FOR YOUNG VIOLINIST screams the headline.

I straighten out the paper and start reading. It quickly becomes obvious that Tarni has read and memorized the entire story – which continues onto pages two and three, with a special feature on page fourteen.

"You've known all this since the gas station?" I ask.

"Yeah," says Tarni. "So what?"

I don't know what to say.

"You said...you said they didn't have newspapers in the gas station. You lied," I blurt out. "All this time... you've been lying to me."

Tarni looks down at the ground.

"Why would you do that? I don't understand."

Tarni says nothing.

"I don't know why you would do that," I shout. I suddenly feel anger rising up in me. "It's not right. It's just NOT RIGHT!"

I throw Debonaire's rucksack over my back, pick up the violin and walk away, the feelings of loneliness suddenly more acute than ever.

I don't know where I am going. I don't even lift my eyes

from my feet. But I feel like I have walked for hours on my own.

Finally, once the tears in my eyes have dried up, I find a small cluster of rocks and sit myself down near them.

I read through the newspaper again but linger on the photograph right in the centre of page fourteen. It is a picture of my mother and my father. At a press conference. They both look upset – it is obvious my mother has been crying. Dad looks tall and solid, his arm round Mum's shoulders. Mum looks like she could fall to the floor at any moment, which is so unlike her. They both wear black.

Page fourteen is a profile of the "missing girl's parents". I sit in the sun and skim read it, realizing that I already know everything it says.

Roy Vanderbolt. Lawyer to the famous. Has represented and advised Hollywood royalty, sports stars and rock stars all around the globe. Lives in a sprawling mansion in the Toorak district of Melbourne, but also has a luxury flat overlooking Sydney Harbour and a house on Hampstead Heath, London. Owns two private planes and a yacht. Keen amateur fisherman.

Delphine Vanderbolt (née Renouf), wife of Roy. Daughter of property magnate Anton Renouf. Australian socialite and interior designer. Founder of three charitable organizations and chairperson for several others. Bronze medallist in cross-country skiing in the 2002 Salt Lake City Winter Olympics. One child, thirteen-year-old Sienna.

All of this I know.

I know everything now.

I remember everything. It is like a waterfall has suddenly opened up on me and I'm trying to catch it all in a plastic cup. I'm not sure how to react.

I fold up the paper and put it on the ground next to me.

I realize I am hungry and thirsty, so I almost finish up one of Debonaire's extra bottles of water and rip open a big packet of Cheezels. I stuff handfuls of the chips into my mouth and swallow them down. Mum never lets me eat Cheezels. Or other things like them. She says I should always eat clean, whatever that means. She always makes sure that Mrs Palin, the cook, makes at least one fresh salad a day. (*Kale and lentil salad. Yuck!*) She says that it's important if I am to be the world's greatest violinist.

I'm not sure why.

Once I've finished, I carefully scrunch up the bag and put it back in the rucksack. This is, after all, sacred land.

I stand up and dust the cheesy powder off my fingers and I look around.

I am on my own.

Surrounded by kilometres and kilometres of hard desert, I am alone.

The afternoon drags on as my feet drag over the land.

I walk and I walk and I see nobody. At one point I come across some of the bushes with the poisonous wild peaches. They look juicy and ripe but I know better than to touch them, so I just walk on.

I wish I hadn't lost my pandanus-leaf hat on the salt pan. The sun is hot and angry and, at times, I struggle to see where I am going.

With nobody to talk to, it's amazing just how silent this vast land is.

So I sing to myself and I keep on.

Left, right, left, right, left, right, left, right, left, right.

I think about the movement in my tired legs and I try to keep the mountains on my right, like Debonaire said.

Left, right, left, right, left.

The blisters on my fingers are coming back. The rubbing of the violin case handle is bringing them up again. So I snap off a spiky leaf from an aloe vera plant and squeeze out the soothing sticky stuff, rubbing it all over my fingers and the sunburnt backs of my arms.

As the sun rolls down towards the land, I start to think about where I am going to spend the night. I climb up into the land leading up to the mountains and manage to spot an ideal place – a small dip in the ground sheltered behind a squarish block of rock. I look around to make sure I am not intruding on any obvious predator's hunting ground, before scrambling down into the ditch and checking that there are no droppings or half-eaten carcasses to be seen.

Something that Tarni always does before setting up camp.

I eat some more of Debonaire's provisions and feel a passing prickle of guilt that I have most of the food in the rucksack and Tarni has very little in her canvas bag. In the end I don't eat much at all.

I shake the water bottle in the hope that it will magically refill itself to the very top. Unsurprisingly, it doesn't. So I ration my sips, knowing that the water has to last me as long as possible.

I decide that the best place to sleep will be at the base of the rock. That way, no cold wind will bite through me in the night.

I am sitting at the base of the rock and realizing just how much I want Tarni to be there with me, when I spot something moving at the top of the ditch.

I squint and can just about make out the shape of an orange-brown snake – *iridescent is the word* – zigzagging over the edge and down, carried along by a small avalanche of shale.

Gwardar, I think, staying calm, and my hand reaches out for some small rocks nearby. I squeeze my fingers round a solid-feeling one and watch as the snake slithers its way round some aywerte bushes, all the while heading towards me.

I can almost feel its eyes watching. Checking me out. Testing me.

Okay, I think. *Just a little nearer and...* I feel the weight of the stone in my hand and I get ready to swing my arm to throw it at the snake and scare it off.

It gets closer and closer and I can almost see its split tongue dancing in and out of its sneery mouth.

Come on. Just a little nearer. I pull back my arm ready. Suddenly—

Whoompf!

A pandanus-leaf hat falls onto the ground next to me.

"COOOOOOEEEEEE!" A loud, familiar noise comes from somewhere up behind me. "COOOOOEEEE! CLEAR OUT, YOU SNEAKY BLUDGER! GO BACK TO YOUR STINKY HOLE AND LEAVE US ALL ALONE!!"

The snake whips round and disappears somewhere over the top of the dip.

I turn and look up.

Tarni is sitting on the top of the rock with her legs dangling over the edge above me. She points to the pandanus-leaf hat on the ground beside me.

"You might need that tomorrow. Gonna be a scorcher, I reckon."

The blood in my veins pulses through me, suddenly excited at seeing her. I want to shout up and tell her so.

However, I decide to play it cool. I still want her to know how annoyed I've been with her. I still want to punish her. I think that's the selfish side of me.

I turn back to my original position and talk to her without actually looking at her.

"You found me then," I say, my voice not giving away the delight I feel at seeing her again.

"Never left you," she answers back, just as stony-voiced. "It's just that sometimes you didn't see me, and other times I didn't *let* you see me. Anyway," she adds, "you were going in the right direction and you seemed to be doing okay, so I let you be."

"Oh, thank you *so* much," I say. "I am *so* honoured."

"No need to be like that," Tarni replies sadly and all of my pretend coldness is washed away.

"Oh, Tarni. I'm sorry," I say.

"'S okay."

We sit there in silence for a long time. Me on the ground. Tarni in the air above me.

"You see," Tarni says at last. "I *was* going to tell you. About who you were. A couple of days after the gas station." She shifts her position and some tiny stones fall like rain around me. "Keeping a secret's pretty hard, you know. That's what I realized. It's like dragging a dead kangaroo around with you all the time. A dead kangaroo that just gets heavier and heavier and heavier, and stinkier and stinkier and stinkier. It ain't nice."

"It's the opposite of what I've been doing," I reply. "You've been hiding things inside you, and I've been trying to dig things out."

"Yeah. I suppose," says Tarni before continuing. "I *was* going to tell you. It was all going round in my head and I couldn't get it to stop. It was driving me nuts. So I decided I was going to tell you everything and show you the paper. But then we saw the helicopters."

I twist round and look up at her, the worn undersides of her sandals above my head.

"You see, I knew that the helicopters weren't after *me*. I knew that they were looking for *you*. And it made me angry."

271

"Why?"

"Because you were the lost city girl. The *rich* lost city girl and everyone was out looking for you. The police. The government. The newspapers. *Everyone*." I try to see her face but it is too much in shade from this angle. "But whenever someone from *my* community leaves… whenever a First Country person disappears, the authorities just say they've gone walkabout. Nobody looks for them. Nobody worries."

"Do you mean Brindabel?" I ask, but Tarni doesn't hear me.

"The police don't care. They just wanna sit in their air-conditioned police stations with their feet on the table, watching TV and drinking their coffees."

"I don't understand. Why?"

"Because the world's unfair. You won't see it sat in your luxury apartment overlooking Sydney Harbour, but down here…out here in the middle of the red dust, you see it every day. Some people are more important than other people, I suppose."

"That's rubbish," I spit. "Everyone's the same. Nobody's better than anyone else." I think back to the horrible things I'd said to people like Figgy Day in the past and I shudder a little.

"Try telling that to the authorities," says Tarni. "Look

at the Stolen Generations. If the world was a perfect place, we would all be the same. But it's not. So we ain't."

"Then the world's messed up. The world's wrong. It needs to be put right."

"Yeah."

I turn myself round and lie on my back, staring up at Tarni silhouetted against the fading blue sky.

"After you saw the helicopters, you changed your mind about telling me?"

"Kinda," says Tarni. "I suppose I was jealous. Of you. So, I swallowed my voice and buried my secret even deeper."

Even from this angle I can see that she looks embarrassed.

"I'm not proud of it," she says. "I mean, it didn't help you and it didn't help me. But that's what I did." She shrugs before pausing for a minute. "And, anyway, I liked having you with me."

"What?"

Tarni wipes her nose with the back of her wrist. "Out here. In the bush. It's a big place. Lots of space. I don't normally come out here on my own. Normally I'm with my sister. But without her…well…I felt kinda…lonely, I suppose. It wasn't the same." I shade my eyes against the sky and I can just about make out Candelabra's cage on the rock next to Tarni. "So when I found you...it felt good. I had someone to be here with. Someone to help me." I think she is smiling. "And then there was all that cobblers with the Drongos and...well...I began to realize that I couldn't do this without you. I didn't *want* to let you go." She shuffles on the ledge. "You were my new... my new yaye, in a way. And I wanted you with me."

I nod to myself. "I understand. I still think you should have told me. I still think you should have ended all the worry that I had going round my head. But I understand."

Tarni begins to stand up.

"Where are you going?" I ask.

"I'm coming down," she replies. "To you. We've still got a song to create."

Later in the evening, after we have worked out the next section of the song and eaten some more of Debonaire's food, we both lie under the rug watching the stars peep out from under their own dark blanket.

"So, who *are* you, Sienna Marie Silke Martha Vanderbolt?" asks Tarni, staring up at the sky.

"You read the paper, didn't you?" I say. "You know all about me."

"Papers don't say monkeys," she says. "They just tell you

the things they want you to know. Twist things round so you think the way they do. They don't bother with the real stuff. They keep all the real stuff hidden away, so you think everything's big and flashy and different and you want to find out more and join in. Then you buy more papers and on it goes. Round and round like a rainbow snake eating its own tail." She makes a funny strangled sort of noise. "Hate papers. And magazines. Horrible things."

She rolls onto her side, digs her elbow into the ground and rests her head on her palm.

"No, I wanna know who you are. *Really*. I wanna know something about you that the papers wouldn't know. Or care about. Tell me."

"Okay." I think for a minute. "I'm thirteen. My birth date is August the 27th. I go to a private school in Melbourne. A girls' school."

"Who're your best friends?"

"Hmm?"

"Your friends. Who are they? What're their names?"

"Erm…well, I usually sit next to a girl called Audrey. Audrey Perkins."

"She your best mate?"

"Well…"

"She go round to yours after school? At the weekend? You hang out together?"

"Not…really, no. In fact, I don't think I've ever had anyone from school back to my house."

Tarni squishes up her face in amazement. "Why not?"

"Because I'm too busy." *I'm also not that friendly,* I think, but keep that to myself.

"Busy?"

I sigh. "Every morning – before I go to school – I spend an hour and a half practising my scales on the violin. Just scales. Nothing else. On Monday, Wednesday and Friday, after school, Madame Petrovsky…" I pause for a second and think of my poor, brave violin teacher – herself a well-known and successful violinist in her youth – before continuing. "Madame Petrovsky would come to the house and help me with my pieces."

"You'd have violin lessons?"

"Yes. For two-and-a-half hours."

"Three times a week?"

"Yes. On Tuesday, after school, I have a two-hour piano lesson with Mr Berkoff, followed by a maths tutorial with Ms Dennis. On Thursday, after school, I have a singing lesson with Mrs Brookes – she teaches singing at the university near us – then a French tutorial with Monsieur Leblanc."

"Jeez."

"That's not to mention the two hours of actual violin

practice I have to squeeze in each day."

"What about the weekend? You must get some time free at the weekend, surely?"

"On Saturday, I spend the whole day at the Melbourne Junior Conservatoire."

"What's that?"

"It's like a music college for young people."

"Music again?" Tarni's mouth is wide.

"Yes. I have extra lessons and play in some small chamber groups and an orchestra."

"You must have some friends in the orchestra?"

"Not really. Because my dad is famous and the *Karpilowsky* is so precious – it belongs to us, by the way, it's not on loan – the insurance company insists that between lessons I have to be in a locked room away from everyone else. So I don't really get to spend time with anyone."

"That's real rough."

"Then, on Sunday, I have a swimming lesson – in our pool – in the morning. Practise the violin and piano before lunch. And, in the afternoon, I'm usually rehearsing with one of the major Australian orchestras. I've got concertos lined up with a number of them this year."

Tarni looks horrified. "You ever get time to even sleep?"

"Ha!" I laugh.

"Isn't all that child cruelty or something?"

"My mother's quite pushy. She won a medal skiing at the Olympics, you see. She always says that to be successful you need to work harder than everybody else put together and squared."

"But you're only thirteen."

"Mum's got a fifteen-year plan for me." I brush some grit off my cheek. "I started the violin when I was five. Finished all of my grades by ten. Got my Associate Diploma last year. By sixteen, I should be at the Julliard School in New York, studying under one of the best violinists in the world. While I'm there, I hope to win a number of international competitions – the Klein, Yehudi Menuhin, Paganini. Then I'll move on to major concertos with the world's best orchestras. By the time I'm twenty. That's the plan, anyway."

"That's a lot of pressure," says Tarni looking at me. "A *lot* of pressure."

"Mmm."

We lie there and watch some shooting stars streak across the cold and clear night sky.

"But what about *you*...er...Sienna?" says Tarni. My name sounds strange coming from her lips.

"What about me?"

"Is that *your* plan too? Do you really want to do all that?"

I think. "I suppose," I say. "I've never really thought that hard about it."

"I mean, do you even *like* playing the violin?"

"Of course I do. I love it. And I'm very good at it. Well…technically, anyway."

"What does that mean, 'technically'?" asks Tarni.

"It means my actual technique – the way I play the violin – is brilliant. But Madame Petrovsky says…" I correct myself. "Madame Petrovsky *used* to say that my playing lacked heart. She'd say that I couldn't engage emotionally with the music."

"Yeah, well…" Tarni nods. "You know the reason for that, doncha?"

"What?"

"You're locked in rooms all day. You've spent so long fiddling with the fiddle that you've forgotten that there's a life away from it." Tarni shifts her position a little. "Look," she says wisely. "To understand life you've got to get muck under your fingernails. It's the only way. I mean, if you wanna know what pain is, scrape your knees on a rock. If you wanna know what fear is, get chased by a dingo."

"Or a Drongo," I add.

"Yeah. True." She carries on. "If you wanna know what happiness is, climb to the top of the biggest gumtree around. If you wanna know what greatness is, just lie on your back and stare at the stars." She points upwards. "And if you wanna know what love is, get yourself a best friend. And if you do those things, I'll bet you a trillion dollars that you'll become a better violin player."

I don't say anything.

I just lie on my back and stare at the stars.

At the point when I am just about to slip off to sleep, Tarni suddenly says something, waking me up again.

"Look," she says. "I've been thinking. I know your name is Sienna. And it's a real nice name. A real pretty name. But...well...I'm finding it hard to call you Sienna."

"Why's that?" I ask.

"I dunno. Perhaps it's because firstly you were Moonflower. Then you were Magpie. And then, with Debonaire, you became Maestro. I kinda see you as a little bit of all three, I suppose. And even though I've known your real name for a real long time – and never told you – now that I have to say it...well...it feels wrong to me." She turns as if she's said something that might upset me. "I don't mean to say that to everyone else you can't be Sienna. It's not *that* wrong. It's just wrong *for me.*"

"It's okay," I reassure her. "I understand. *Things like your name, they're just details really.*"

"Eh?"

"That's what you said to me. In the cave when we were sheltering from the sandstorm. *Things like your name, they're just details.*"

"Did I say that?" Tarni smiles. "That's real wise of me."

"You're a very wise person," I say. I sit up and wrap my arms round my legs. "Tarni. I don't care what you call me. Call me Moonflower. Call me Magpie. Call me Maestro. Call me whatever. It doesn't matter. The combination of sounds you put together is irrelevant. I am just me, whatever somebody calls me. And you are you. And the only thing that truly matters is that I like you and you like me – I hope. Beyond that, it wouldn't matter if I had ten arms and a head made of ice cream. It wouldn't matter if you had butterfly wings and rubber balls for knees. None of it would matter. We are friends and nothing should stop us being so."

Tarni grins. "I wish you *did* have a head made of ice cream. At least you would keep me cool."

I smile. "And if you had butterfly wings you could carry us to Karlu Karlu."

Tarni shakes her head. "No way. If we flew then we couldn't write the song." Her eyes look intense. "And I want to write the song more than anything. With you."

I reach over and squeeze her hand. Surprisingly, she squeezes mine back.

"You know," says Tarni. "I don't want to call you Sienna. And I don't want to call you Moonflower, Magpie or Maestro. Not any more. They were good names, but they ain't right. Not now."

"So, what *are* you going to call me?" I ask.

"Tidda," she says. "It means 'best female friend'."

I think about the word. "Tidda. Sounds good. Tidda and Tarni."

"Tidda and Tarni." She laughs. "Tarni and Tidda."

"Tidda and Tarni. Tarni and Tidda," I join in and we chant our names over and over together until we can laugh no more and the fireflies round the embers have given up on us.

Chapter Eighteen
THE RIGHT DECISION

The following morning, the land grows even greener and we cut across a cattle station with hundreds of Brahman cows clustering around patches of buffalo grass. At one point we stop to wash ourselves off in one of the open rainwater tanks that dot across the ranch before pushing on once again.

As we walk, I have a strange sense. Not for the first time. It is as though someone or something is watching us. I don't understand it and I don't say anything to Tarni, but I have a feeling that she feels it too.

Later, as we move into the afternoon, we stop and watch a flock of pink-chested galahs – at least a thousand of them – flying in figures of eight and infinity across the sky. It is an amazing sight. Altogether they remind me of the cluster of bellbirds that flew into the path of the plane just before it crashed, and I find myself wondering if Candelabra had been one of them…

As we try and find somewhere to camp for the night, I notice Tarni staring at me. She looks serious again, like she is about to reveal some other secret she has on me.

"What is it?" I ask.

"Well. You know…" she says, "now that you remember who you are…and you can remember who your ma and pa are…well…shouldn't you…?" She doesn't finish off the sentence.

And it's true. Ever since our argument, when everything about me came rushing back, I'd been thinking the same thing. The picture of Dad supporting Mum in the newspaper. Mum's tear-streaked face. Shouldn't I find my way back home to them? As soon as possible? Isn't that what I should do?

After all, I do miss them. Dad with his silly jokes and endless business meetings. Mum with her strict, decisive, orderly mind and a determination for me to succeed at all costs.

I do miss them.

I *have* missed them.

But then I remember the dream of being trapped in

the tower, watching all the children below having fun. A life behind glass. Like a pinned butterfly. Hidden away. Protected.

And I think of the selfish, sarcastic girl I am – or, at least, have been. Happy to leave Figgy Day crying over a marble.

And I look at my friend Tarni – *my friend!* And I see the worries on her face. Still believing she murdered that man. Still secretly frightened that she won't catch up with her sister. Still feeling that she needs me with her.

And I think about the song that we are creating.

"No." I smile. "I love my parents very, very much, and I'm pretty certain they love me. I don't want them to suffer any more than they have to. Of course not. But… At the moment, after everything we've been through, I think it's right to put *you* first. I want to help you find Brindabel. I want to be there when you find her. We've come this far. I don't think a few more days is going to make much of a difference. Not now."

Tarni reaches over and kisses me on the forehead. "Thank you, Tidda."

And the glow I feel keeps me floating all evening.

The song is growing.

When Tarni sings and I play, it is like we are just one person. The same person. Not two. We both seem to instinctively feel what the other is about to do. We are mirror images of each other.

When I am playing the song, I think about my friend. Tarni. I think about everything we've been through together and how I feel about her. It is almost as if my mind has no control over my fingers.

It is my *heart* that plays.

It is a way that I have never played before.

And I like it.

Madame Petrovsky would be proud.

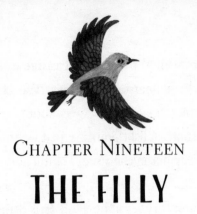

CHAPTER NINETEEN
THE FILLY

We walk for an entire morning. Over the red desert, past small clusters of gumtrees, through wide seas of swaying green grass. We climb to the brim of a very round hill and when we finally arrive at the top...

"Get down!" Tarni's hand grabs my shoulder and forces me to my knees. "Look!"

On the other side of the hill...

The white Jeep judders along slowly. Smoke coming out of its exhaust.

"It's them!" cries Tarni. "I mean, it's *her*. She's still after me for doing her son in."

We lie down flat on our bellies so that she can't see us.

"She's out for blood. I told you, didn't I?" says Tarni, a nervous look on her face. "I can sense it."

On the front of the bonnet I can see a dull red stain from where the kangaroo had been strapped. Then I spot something else...

"What's that?" I ask, pointing just behind the Jeep.

Tarni shades her eyes to see.

"Oh no..."

As the truck turns on the sand and comes to a stop, it becomes obvious.

A horse – dark-coated, spindly-legged, young, exhausted – walks behind the Jeep, tied by a length of thick rope to the bumper.

"What *is* she doing with a foal?" I say.

But Tarni doesn't say anything. She just shakes her head.

The Jeep stops shivering and hisses itself still.

We tuck ourselves down tighter to the ground and watch as the left-hand door opens and the old woman, in the same ridiculous leather hat, steps out. Even from this distance I can see that she is almost having trouble breathing. She leans onto the bonnet and looks around. It is obvious that she hasn't seen us.

"Oh no. Do you think she's copped us?" Tarni whispers.

"No," I reply. "I don't. Now shush." I am surprised at how scared Tarni sounds.

"I'm sure she's hunting me down."

"Ssh!"

"Wants to get me back for popping him off."

Then I realize something.

"She's not driving," I say.

"What?"

"She's not driving. She got out of the wrong door. Somebody else is driving."

Tarni looks me up and down like I am mad. Then she turns back to the Jeep.

"Oh, this is hopeless," the old woman krarks in her terrible rasping voice and the noise carries up the hill towards us. "I said you shouldn't have come this way."

The driver's door opens and out pokes the head of the woman's son. Bobby. Professor Drongo!

Tarni makes a tiny noise like a yelp or a squeak.

"Don't blame me. It's not my fault. You were the one who was meant to change the tyres," says Professor Drongo over the top of his door. "Anyway, it's the wrong type of sand."

"He's not dead," says Tarni, grinning. "He's not dead!"

"Of course he's not," I say as we both notice him rubbing the top of his sore shoulder with his hand. "You didn't kill him."

"*Wrong type of sand!*" screams the mother. "How can it be the wrong type of sand?" She slams her door shut and makes her way round to the horse they are towing. She grabs its badly fitting head collar and yanks the poor creature's head round. "The nag needs watering," she shouts.

"What?" calls her son, climbing out of the driver's seat.

"The nag needs water." Then she seems to turn her attention to the horse, putting on a weird and slightly scary voice. "*Doncha, my beauty. Never gonna be a Melbourne Cup winner if we don't keep you watered and fed, eh?*" She slaps the side of the horse and it jumps in fear. "*If we can't get rich saving some spoilt brat with a fiddle, we're gonna get rich with you. You're our little back-up plan.*"

I hear Tarni growl right next to me and I find my fists suddenly clenched.

"There's a freshwater cattle trough," says the son, pointing into the far-off distance. I squint and can just about make out a long metal tank glinting in the light. "We can take it there."

"Probably won't make it that distance," says the mother. "Probably die before we get there. C'mon." She opens the back door and pulls out a big, clear plastic water carrier. "Grab one of these. We're running low and we're going to have to walk it."

The son doesn't look too happy, reaching in and taking a military green container before slamming his own door.

"Easier to just put a bullet in it and leave it for the birds to pick at." He coughs as they set off. "A lot quicker too."

Tarni and I watch them as they both slowly – very, *very* slowly – make their way across the flat plain towards the water tank.

After a while, we look at each other. They hadn't spotted us, so it would be easy for us to just creep back down the hill and take a different route. It would be so easy to just...disappear. And there is an enormous temptation to do just that. Slip away silently. Invisibly. Without fuss.

But...and we are both clearly thinking the same thing...we can't.

"We can't just leave the brumby there with them," says Tarni. "They won't take good enough care of...her... him. Be dead by the time they're finished."

"She's a filly," I say, looking down at her.

"How can you tell?"

"I just can," I reply. "What do they want with her anyway? Surely they don't believe they can train her to become a racehorse, do they?"

"Ha! They couldn't train each other to do up their own shoelaces," says Tarni. "All I know is that we can't leave her with them."

"We need to get her to safety. We need to set her free," I agree, my eye catching the green of Candelabra's wing reaching out through the bars of his cage, before Tarni and I both nod at each other.

We wait for the man and the woman to get about three quarters of the way to the water trough before we move. Leaving behind our bags, the violin and Candelabra, we race down the hill to the Jeep. The filly looks up at us, her eyes bright with fear.

"Hey. Hey," says Tarni, holding her arms out in front of her. "It's okay... It's okay... Do you know much about horses? I don't know all that much about horses."

"Wait," I say. "Let me."

I walk slowly in front of Tarni and, keeping my voice low, I say, "Hello, beautiful."

The filly's eyes widen even more and she looks as if she is about to pull away from me. So I move even slower, stepping cautiously into her space. "Shush now, my lovely." I smile and reach up to take hold of the rope that binds her to the back of the Jeep. "There, there."

I lean my head in closer and sigh softly towards her. She breathes me in, and I breathe her in and we stay there for a short time, just taking each other's breaths in and building the trust.

I sense her calming.

"Cool," says Tarni. "So cool."

"It's all going to be okay," I say to the filly. "We're going to get you away from these people. You're going to be free again."

My hand slides along the rope to the place where it is tied to the back of the white Jeep. I tug at the knot, but it is too tight.

"Let me," says Tarni, who steps in slowly and, after a few seconds, holds up the end of the rope. "There."

I take it from her before stroking the foal on her neck. "That's right. Come with *me* now. It's time to go."

I pull the rope and she starts to move. I lead her up the hill, her weak legs half buckling with the effort.

"She needs water," I say to Tarni.

"I haven't got much left," replies Tarni, marching ahead of us.

"Give her mine," I say.

"But *you* haven't got much left."

"Doesn't matter. Give her mine."

Tarni races to the top of the hill and starts scrummaging around in the bags. As the filly and I reach her, I can see that she has poured some of my water out into her wooden bowl.

"Here we are, girl," says Tarni, holding out the bowl.

The filly leans in and sucks up the water in no time.

"Give her it all," I say. "Don't leave any for me."

Tarni tips the clear plastic bottle until it is empty and holds the bowl out for the filly once again. She puts her small nose in and drains it, licking the empty wooden bottom.

Tarni shakes her head. "She's thirsty...so thirsty..." Bending over her canvas bag, Tarni pulls out her own bottle, removes the top and empties it into the bowl. "She needs it more than me right now."

The filly drinks it all up and I can see that her eyes look more trusting of us.

"We need to go," I say, looking across the flat lands behind us. "Before they get back and see what we've done."

Tarni shades her eyes against the sun. "They're ages away. We've got a good head start. Come on."

We stumble back the way we came, then take a slightly different route. All the while trying to keep small hillocks, sand dunes and trees between us and the Jeep.

The filly walks better now that she is a little refreshed and knows that we are not going to hurt her. Once or twice she snickers, so I run my hand over her velvety coat and pat her on the neck.

"Don't tell me," says Tarni. "Your ma is an expert horse rider. Won a gold medal in horse riding in some big competition or other. Am I right? Taught you how to ride."

"Sort of," I say, keeping the lead rope taut. "Used to be around horses a lot when I was little. Before I started the violin. Before Mum realized that *that* was the skill she needed to push. These days I'm not allowed to ride so much, as I might fall off and damage my hand. Endanger my future career."

I see Tarni shaking her head and I find myself shaking my head along with her.

Suddenly, there is a bang somewhere far off behind us. The filly jumps, but I keep a strong, tight hold on her rein.

"Sssh. Ssssssssh," I soothe. "Calm down." Thankfully she does.

"What was that?" says Tarni. "Are they shooting at us again?"

"Didn't sound like that," I say.

"Wait here." Tarni runs off to the top of a small stony cliff nearby and stares into the distance. After a few seconds, she waves at me to join her. So I tie the end of the lead rein to a branch on a dead and bent-over tree before climbing up to see.

"Look!"

I stare back across the land over which we've just walked. Far away, like a small white dot on the horizon, I can see the Jeep. And snaking its way out of the front of the Jeep is a tall pillar of twisty black smoke. There are flames too.

"Looks like even their truck has got fed up with them," says Tarni. "Engine's gone and blown up. Bang! That's one dead Jeep they've got there. I don't think they're going anywhere in a hurry."

"You think they might follow us on foot?" I ask.

"I don't think they're capable. They would have got too exhausted just walking to the water trough and back. Probably need a good lie-down, the poor things."

"You think they'll be all right? Out here on their own." I feel a tiny bit concerned for them. "Stranded like that. What if they die?"

"Don't worry, Tidda," says Tarni. "I've got a feeling they'll be just fine. They just won't be going anywhere for a while, that's all. Cheerio, Drongos!"

The filly feeds from the rich patches of grass that grow around here. So much more lush and fat than the sprouts of spiky aywerte that still occasionally dot over our path. After a while, we come across another cattle trough, being fed from pipes that hiss under the brown earth. We all drink deeply and refill the bottles, before resting a little in the shade of a nearby tree. Tarni opens Candelabra's cage door and, lifting him out, puts him on top of my head once again.

"I wish you wouldn't do that."

Tarni laughs. "He loves it. Feels right at home on top of your nut."

As if to show his agreement, Candelabra does his incredibly ear-piercing call – partly deafening me and spooking the filly – and flaps his wings, strengthening them out.

We both keep laughing.

Almost as a joke we try some of Debonaire's wattleseed bread, and are surprised to find that it is one of the most delicious things we've ever eaten. Like ambrosia. In fact, we have to force ourselves to stop eating it. Occasionally I pull a tiny piece off, hold it above my head and feed it to Candelabra, who seems to appreciate it as much as we do.

Then we push on, safe and happy in the knowledge that the Drongos are nowhere near.

"You know," says Tarni, "it's obvious I couldn't have killed him. Daft to think I had. I mean… I'm a good shot but… Well…" Her relief is obvious. "Let's just say I'm pleased I didn't kill him."

"Yes." I think back to a time – just a few days before – when I was worried that I'd stolen the violin and was capable of murder. Strange now to think that such an idea could dominate my thoughts.

As the sun crawls across the sky and starts to lower itself on the other side, the filly stops.

"Come on," I say and tug on the rope. But she doesn't move.

"What's wrong with her?" asks Tarni.

Then the filly neighs.

"What is it, girl?" I whisper.

Then she neighs again. And again. And again.

"Sssh."

"Look," says Tarni, pointing.

I turn.

Standing next to some coolabah trees far off across the plain is another dark horse. Watching us.

"It's her mother," I say, and just as I say it, the mare in the distance neighs back.

"She's been following all the time, hasn't she?" Tarni nods. "Following the Drongos, then following us. She's come to get her."

The filly strains at the rope and I struggle to hold onto her.

"Whoa!"

"You've got to let her go," says Tarni. "Take that stupid head collar thing off and let her go, Tidda."

I hold on even tighter for a second, a part of me not wanting to set her free. A part of me wanting to keep her for ever. Make her mine.

"Tidda," Tarni looks at me. "Let her go."

I look across at the mare, neighing, and for a split moment I remember Madame Petrovsky waving at me across the concert hall foyer. Calling me on. And I think about the invisible eyes that I have felt watching over Tarni and me for so long now.

And then I think about the giant marble that I took from Figgy Day, making her cry...

So I slip the clip off the head collar, pull it away and stand back.

The filly walks off without looking back and then, as the distance between the two horses lessens, she breaks into a gallop. Her hooves pounding the earth in excitement.

Tarni and I stand there watching as the filly and mare nod their greetings to each other, before turning and disappearing into the glowing heat haze.

"We never gave her a name," says Tarni. "We should have given her a name."

I shake my head. "She didn't need one," I reply, feeling both sad and happy at the same time.

After a chilly and restless night – in which neither of us sleeps at all – I get up awkwardly and straighten my limbs. I stretch the stiffness out and then pull down some wild peaches from a nearby bush for breakfast. As I take them down I am suddenly hit with a realization.

Soon I will be home.

But the thought of it doesn't *completely* fill me with happiness.

Which is weird.

Because I think I am beginning to miss this outside life already. A life without so many of the things we take for granted. No phones or computers. No trains or cars. No glitzy disco ball hair salons or sticky bubble waffle bars.

Just the land.

A beautiful and brutal land. Relentless and endless. Empty yet full. Where the songs sung are the songs of life, and the music played is the music of the stars.

Now, at last, I understand Tarni's love for her country.

I roll a wild peach in my hand and feel its softness. No peach I ever had in Melbourne ever *felt* so soft. I hold it up to my nose and sniff. No peach I ever had in Melbourne ever *smelt* so good. I put it up to my lips. Then I bite. No peach I ever had in Melbourne ever *tasted* so—

"Wait!" Tarni shouts and the suddenness of the noise

makes the piece of peach drop out from my mouth onto one of my boots.

Tarni laughs.

"What are you doing?" I shout.

Tarni grins. "Tidda. It's lucky one of us has been paying attention as we travel and not just daydreaming about Tchaikovsky's hundredth didgeridoo concerto or whatever."

"What are you on about?"

"Do you wanna be sick again? Do you wanna be caught doing thirty goonas before lunchtime?"

I look at the rest of the peach in my hand.

"Oh," I say.

"Yes," says Tarni. "I wouldn't eat any more of that if you wanna keep your guts where they currently are."

I throw the "peach" into the middle of a spiky-looking bush.

A beautiful land this might be. But it's also pretty treacherous.

And I'm not sure I'm completely suited to it.

Chapter Twenty
THE HOTEL

Time passes. How much, I don't know. It feels like there's no real difference between the hours and the days and the weeks now. They all blur into one another. Just like the distances we walk. I do not know if I have walked one kilometre or ten. Whatever strength I have left in my legs cannot tell. My judgement of these things seems to have vanished.

So we just keep on walking.

Then we see the telegraph poles.

A whole line of them standing upright in the dust, five lengths of sagging wires linking them all together. Like a musical stave. Birds perched along them like notes.

"And where there are telegraph poles," says Tarni, "there's usually a road."

We walk over the uneven land, past the clusters of

gumtrees towards the poles. Sure enough, just beyond them lies a road.

"The Stuart Highway," says Tarni as we step out onto the grey tarmac. She points to the left where the road disappears into a heat haze. "Starts *way way* down near the ocean in the south and then –" she points in the opposite direction – "goes on all the way to Darwin in the north. About three thousand kilometres. Cuts the entire country in two."

For such a long and important road, the Stuart Highway doesn't seem like anything special. Just two dull, flat lanes – one leading north, one leading south – with a dotted white line along its centre.

And there is no traffic to be seen.

"Which way?" I ask, looking up and down the road.

Tarni tugs out Debonaire's map and turns her back to the sun to read it in shade.

"We're a little south of Karlu Karlu. Probably about four or five kilometres, I reckon." She pushes the paper back into her dungarees pocket and nods her head to the north. "So…this way." Tarni marches off.

It is strange walking on a real road after all this time. It feels too solid. Too easy. After having to push against dust and grit and sand and salt – all of which make your legs tired – walking along this road feels like bouncing along a long, straight trampoline.

In fact, walking along the road is tedious. Much more tedious than walking over the desert. With the desert, the landscape is always changing. One moment you are walking along a flat stretch with hardly any vegetation. The next you are dragging yourself up a hill through thick tufts of grass. After that you might be edging your way along the bank of a dried-up riverbed or skirting around a tepid billabong or crossing a small salt pan. It might have taken some time, but I have come to realize that the outback is a beautiful, ever-changing thing.

Unlike the road.

The road is *truly* endless. Each stretch of it looks the same as the one before. Straight, grey, monotonous and dull. Out of boredom I start to count the telegraph poles that run alongside the highway like tall pins holding the edge of the desert in position.

After about three hundred I give up.

The afternoon is hot. The air is oddly misty.

And Tarni doesn't talk. Her eyes are focused on the road like she is willing it to give up some secret. So I stay quiet too.

Eventually, we spot a low, flat building in the distance, just to the side of the road. As we get nearer we can see a large, brightly painted sign beside it.

THE GIANT'S MARBLES HOTEL, it reads in bulbous bubbly lettering.

"That's it," says Tarni, speeding up a little. "That's the place Debonaire mentioned."

We walk onto the short service road for the hotel, past four or five burnt-out old trucks. I stare at them as we pass. It is strange. They almost look like they haven't just been abandoned there. It is like they've been neatly lined up, placed perfectly alongside one another, like a work of art.

The hotel itself looks like it is made from corrugated iron sheets and plastic, and has three or four palm trees out front, clearly designed to make it appear more sophisticated than it truly is. Some old-fashioned chrome gas and diesel pumps gleam in the sunlight and a swirly lettered sign propped up against a wall tells potential customers that *Gas. Accommodation. Hot Dogs. And Juke Box!* are available here.

I glance across at Tarni. She looks worried.

"You okay?" I ask.

She puts on one of her tough faces and smiles. "Sure!" she says.

We cross the tarmac and push open the glass door into reception.

Inside it feels cool – the loud swish of a ceiling fan can be heard above our heads – and it looks dark. I realize that having been out in the bright light for so long, my eyes will take time to adjust to being inside. So, after a couple of seconds I can still only just about make out a tall leafy green pot plant in one corner of the room, a small pink sofa with a stack of dusty old magazines teetering on a stumpy table next to it, and a long lime-green Formica counter behind which stands a youngish woman with really big hair and a lot of bright make-up on her face.

"Hi there. Oh." She stops. "I'm afraid we don't allow animals in the hotel." She points down at Candelabra in his cage. "Could you possibly leave it just outside the door? Please?"

Tarni sighs. "*Him*. Not *it*," she mutters to herself, but she opens the glass door again and puts Candelabra just the other side of it.

There is another noise in the reception area and it takes me a short time to figure out what it is. Behind the counter, a tiny flickering ancient television is hissing static to itself.

"Now, how can I help you both? You here with your parents?"

"Er…no," I say, feeling nervous. Worried that the woman might recognize me from the papers or the television. Worried she might want to call the police and claim the reward for my safe return, like the Drongos. Worried Tarni and I might never get to the end of our journey.

"No. We're not with our parents." Tarni looks serious. "I'm following my sister. Somebody told me my sister might have passed through here."

The woman frowns. "Did they?"

"Yes." Tarni doesn't leave any gap in the conversation. "I was hoping she might be here." She sounds more nervous than I feel.

"Ah!" The woman's face switches in a moment like she has suddenly remembered. "Yes. Of course. You must be Tarni."

Tarni looks shocked. "Yes. I am."

"Your sister said you might come looking for her."

"Is she here? Where is she?" Excitement in her voice. "Could you go and get her for me, please? Could you tell her I'm here?"

The receptionist shakes her head. "Oh, she's not here now."

"What?"

"Of course she's not. She's gone." Her face is serious. "But…oh yes. She left something for you."

The woman turns and walks into a room behind the reception.

Tarni doesn't say anything. Neither do I. Apart from the dull rumble of the fan, the only sound is that of the television in the corner, which has somehow started babbling to itself.

So, Waid, says the prim and upright female newsreader on the stuttering black-and-white screen. *What can you tell us about Tarni Woll?*

Hearing Tarni's name, we both look up.

The picture cuts to a stiff, slick-haired man in a stiff, slick-cut suit – dark tie tightly squeezed up to the place where his chin starts and his neck ends – holding a retro-looking microphone in front of his polished face. He is standing outdoors somewhere, in front of some flat, square-shaped buildings.

Mimi, says the man in a crisp, clipped voice. *I'm here in the middle of the Northern Territory. The red centre of Australia. A rugged, uncompromising, beautiful land.* He starts to walk slowly, never once taking his eyes off the camera that's filming him. *And I've come here to one of the Utopia outstations to meet Jedda Woll – Tarni Woll's mother.*

I look at Tarni and see that she is also staring at the screen, so I turn back to it.

The man walks until he is alongside a First Country woman in her late thirties. She looks frightened.

"Ma!" Tarni says.

Mrs Woll. It is the voice of the reporter, Waid. *Tell us all about Tarni.*

Tarni's mother looks directly at the camera and talks. *Well. Tarni is thirteen years old. She goes to school here in the Utopia outstation. And she ran away from home after her sister went. I don't know why. I think she was upset.*

The reporter nods and puts on a fake face of concern. *And how did that make you feel, Mrs Woll?*

Tarni's mother shakes her head. *Sad. I am missing her. My home hasn't been right without her. It has felt empty and cold. And I don't like it.* She takes a breath and looks as though she is trying not to cry. *Come home, Tarni,* she says straight into the lens of the camera. *Come home, please. Come home.*

The reporter barely notices the mother's pain. *So, Mrs Woll. What kind of things does Tarni—*

Come home, Tarni, says her mum, ignoring the reporter completely. *Please come home.* A single tear runs down her cheek.

I turn to Tarni and notice that her eyes are filled with water.

"What's she think she's doing?" says Tarni. "Being...
filmed like that. It ain't right."

I am stunned. I don't know what to say, so I say
nothing. Tarni also says nothing, but I see her nodding
to herself.

On the television, the news has already been replaced
by a screen full of static and white noise once again.

"Here we are." The receptionist comes back behind
the counter. "Your sister left *this* for you." She holds out
an envelope.

"Not another letter?" cries Tarni. "Why's she always
leaving me letters?"

She takes the envelope and rips it apart. Inside is a
single leathery sheet of paper. Tarni unravels it and reads.
A second or two later she turns it round so I can see.

On the paper, written in large blocky capitals are the
words:

TARNI. I LOVE YOU. I ALWAYS WILL.
GO BACK HOME.

We sit between the charred remains of what look like
1950s Chevrolets, their rounded bug-shaped cabins still
intact. The sun burns down on the two of us from above

and the plastic hotel shimmers like it has been caught in the middle of the heat haze.

For a long time we don't say very much. We just sit and think. The only sounds, those of the birds that fly high in the sky and the soft, hot breeze that blows around us.

"I wish I hadn't come," says Tarni finally. "Yaye doesn't want me to follow her. She doesn't want me to go wherever she's gone. She's made that clear enough."

I pause for a second before replying.

"But if you hadn't..." I start. "Well, you wouldn't have found Candelabra. You wouldn't have been able to fix him up. He would have been eaten by a snake or a dingo. You saved his life."

Tarni stares at the ground.

"If you hadn't come," I continue, "we wouldn't have been able to rescue the filly...the brumby... She would still be tied to the back of the Drongo's Jeep."

I look at Tarni and I can see her looking at me.

"And if you hadn't tried chasing Brindabel...well, you wouldn't have found *me*." I feel like I don't have to – or want to – say any more.

Tarni nods sadly.

"Yeah. I'm glad I found you. I'm glad you're still here. I'm glad we've done this together. It's just that...well...

I wanted to find...Yaye. Again. Find her and ask her if there was anything I could have done to stop her from going. Tell her that everything is okay. Ask her... Well, stuff like that."

I shrug. "You can't control other people. Nobody can. Not even my mum. All you can do is be you. And be there for them when they need you." I reach over and squeeze Tarni's hand again. She squeezes it back. "It's difficult to do...but sometimes you have to know when to let go." I think back to my reluctance to set the filly free and I realize what a difficult thing that is to do.

Tarni nods again.

She folds the piece of paper with the ten words on it back up and slips it into the pocket on the front of her dungarees. "I know," she says.

CHAPTER TWENTY-ONE

THE SIXTIES

We trudge along the tarmac road, tacking our way towards Karlu Karlu.

"Must have felt strange," I say, wiping the sweat from my forehead. "Seeing your mum on television like that."

"Yeah," says Tarni, still staring at the road before her.

"Must have felt weird. Why do you think they were talking to her on the television?"

But Tarni doesn't answer. She just keeps on walking.

A while later, I look behind and spot a vehicle on the horizon, heading towards us. As it gets closer, I can see that it is a glossy, red people carrier.

Tarni and I stand to the side of the road to let it pass, but when the driver sees us, the car slows and stops.

The passenger window winds down and a woman of about fifty peers out of it.

"You girls all right?" she asks.

"Need a lift?" calls out the man behind the wheel.

"No," I say. "It's okay."

"Where're you headed?" The woman leans a little out of the window to see us.

I look at Tarni expecting her to answer, but she says nothing. She just looks down at the ground.

"Karlu Karlu," I say instead. "The Giant's Marbles."

The man points to his windscreen. "That's just up ahead. We can give you both a lift if you'd like. Stick your bird in the boot." I notice that he wears a sort of white cowboy hat with a sparkly blue band round it.

"That's very kind of you," I reply. "But…I think we want to do it on our own."

The man in the hat looks uncertain. "Are you sure? I mean, it's a helluva walk for two young girlies like yourselves. Coupla kilometres or something."

I turn to Tarni again, expecting to see her smiling. But she isn't. She just stares at the dust beneath our feet like she is a thousand kilometres away from here.

"No. I think we'll be okay. Thank you."

"Where've you come from?" asks the woman, shading her eyes from the sun. "There's nothing for kilometres around here. Where'd you start out?"

I brush the sticky hair from off my head. "Oh. A long way back. But we've been walking all morning. We came out on this road just the other side of the hotel and now we're going on to Karlu Karlu."

"Hotel?" asks the man.

"Yes. The Giant's Marbles Hotel." I point off into the distance behind them. "Back there."

The man shakes his head.

"There's no hotel back there," he says.

"Yes there is," I say, still pointing. "We came past it this morning. In fact, we went into it."

"Uh-huh," says the man. "You must be getting confused. I've lived in this area all my life. I know this land like the back of my elbows, and I can tell you that there's no hotel in that direction. Not for at least another hundred kilometres. Not until you get to Wilora."

The woman turns to face the man. "Didn't there *used* to be a hotel nearby, Karl? I think there used to be one, years ago."

The man thinks. "Yes...you're right, Lou. I remember now. But that burnt down a long time ago. In the sixties, I think. I was barely even born then."

"Well, I suppose someone must have rebuilt it," I say. "It was definitely there just now."

The woman frowns and glances back at the man.

"I...um...I don't think so. We've just come that way ourselves. There's nothing there."

"Never has been," says the man with a worried face. "Well, not since the sixties anyway."

I think back to the hotel. I think back to the receptionist with the big hair, the ancient television, the Formica counter and the sign advertising a jukebox.

The sixties?

"Have you two girlies drunk enough water today?" asks the man, thrusting a plastic bottle in front of his wife's face towards us. "Only, if you don't drink enough water, the brain starts to go bananas. You start imagining things."

My mind is still on the hotel, so I automatically reach up and take the bottle, slipping it into Debonaire's rucksack.

"Perhaps you'd better hitch a ride with us," says the woman. "To the marbles. Might be safest."

Suddenly Tarni seems to come alive. "No!" she almost shouts. "No. Me and Tidda are walking. All the way. On our own. We don't need a lift!"

I smile at the couple. "Thanks anyway," I say, trying to downplay Tarni's outburst. "It's not *that* far."

The woman and the man look at each other as if to say that they'd rather take us to Karlu Karlu themselves.

"Look," says the man. "I tell you what. We'll drive on and let somebody know that you're on your way. That sound fair dinkum?"

"Yes," I reply. "That sounds good. Thank you."

Tarni stares off into the distance, along the road. She doesn't answer the man.

"Okay. We'll do that, then." He restarts the engine of the car. "But be careful. It's a hot afternoon. Make sure you keep yourselves topped up with water, d'you hear?"

"Yes. We will."

The woman looks pityingly at us, like she can't imagine us both surviving the short journey to Karlu Karlu. "Well, you take good care of yourselves now," she says. "And we'll make sure they know you're coming."

"Okay," I nod. "Thank you again."

The woman sticks her thumb up at us and the red SUV suddenly zooms off, quickly disappearing into the flat horizon.

Tarni and I stand there for a while, neither of us saying anything.

Eventually, I turn to Tarni and smile.

"I don't know what all that was about," I say. "I mean, that hotel was *definitely* there this morning, wasn't it?" I laugh nervously. "I mean, I didn't imagine it, did I?"

But Tarni doesn't answer again. Instead, she straightens

the canvas bag on her shoulder, switches Candelabra's cage from one hand to the other and sighs.

"What's wrong?" I ask.

She points her free hand to the road ahead. "I think…" she says. "I think…I think she's nearby."

Chapter Twenty-Two

THE REASON

We walk in silence. Not because I don't want to talk or because I can't think of anything to say. But because it is like Tarni isn't even there.

She strides on. So quickly that I struggle to keep up with her. She pounds her way along the road so fast that I have to burst into a run every now and then just to keep her in sight.

At one point, I notice a pair of long black curves sliding their way along the tarmac, out onto the rough ground at the side of the road. Tyre marks. A short distance into the bush I can make out the remains of the upside-down, burnt-out car that made them – a little like the Chevrolets at the "hotel". Only I can tell from the shape that this is a more modern car. An SUV. An accident that happened months or maybe years ago.

Weeds grow out through the blackened, smashed windows and dust has blown itself into the inside roof of the cabin, so it is almost impossible to know precisely where the desert ends and the car begins.

Looking down at my feet, I can see flowers. Withered and dead – difficult to tell what flowers they once were – tied together with a bleaching yellow bow that shivers in the hot breeze. Attached to the bow is a small rectangular strip of card. Bending down I pull the bow over to one side to see the words written on the card.

Karl & Lou. Mum and Dad. We miss you. Sleep well. P, T and Baby W. XXX

I straighten up and take a step back, feeling as if I have accidentally intruded on somebody's grief.

After what feels like a long time in this corrosive afternoon heat, Tarni stops dead – hypnotized by the sight ahead – and, puffing, I manage to come alongside her.

"Hey," I say. "Is that it?"

The Giant's Marbles.

Karlu Karlu.

Hundreds of massive red boulders – two or three times my height – dotted around the reserve before us, many of them stacked in piles.

Like huge marbles.

"That looks cool," I say, expecting Tarni to agree. "Don't you think?"

Tarni tries to force her face into a smile but fails completely.

"What's wrong?" I ask.

Tarni shakes her head. "Nothing. Come on."

She walks on.

It is strange. The sky is turning dark. Fast. There are clouds above us – thick, grey, rolling clouds that have grown in the sky, giving the air around me a coldness that I haven't experienced before out here in the bush.

I don't like it. It feels almost unnatural.

I don't think Tarni notices the change in the temperature as she makes her way into the reserve. It is like she is mesmerized, so I hold myself back and follow her from a distance. I don't know what she is thinking and I don't really understand what is going on, so I let her lead the way.

She stops next to a large rectangular wooden sign just off the side of the road.

WELCOME TO KARLU KARLU, it shouts in big carved letters.

On the sign, underneath some Perspex casing, is a map of the area next to a pencil sketch of two of the rocks – one rock perched precariously on top of the other, like it could topple off at any moment.

"*This* is why she came here," says Tarni, staring at the board. "When Debonaire said...she was going to Karlu Karlu, I wondered why she was coming here. For a minute, it didn't make sense to me. But then I realized. I remembered."

"What?" I ask. "What do you mean?"

"This." She nods at the sign. "This is the reason. We talked for so long about coming here to see it. It was just a silly idea, really. Just a tiny pretend dream that we had. A joke. But she did it. She came here to see it after all."

I stand next to Tarni and look at the board.

First I scan the map. There is nothing particularly special about it. There is information about the First Country names of some of the rocks and the paths along which to walk. A short history of the area, and a list of all the wildlife that can be found.

Then I look at the pencil sketch poster alongside it.

The rocks are beautiful and detailed – one rock completely dependent on the one beneath it – and... I frown. There is something about the style of it that I recognize. Something familiar. Something that makes me think of paint-flicked stones with horses and hunters on them.

So I peer down in the bottom right-hand corner.

And I see the name of the artist.

Tarni Woll.

"You...*you* drew that?" I ask, pointing at it.

"Yeah."

"It's...great," I say.

"'S okay."

"It's brilliant! When did you do it?"

She answers me like she doesn't really want to answer me. "Ages ago. In school. It was a competition. It was a *national* competition." She says *national* like it carries twenty tonnes.

"And you won?"

Tarni nods, not taking her eyes from the poster. "I won the school a big box of books."

I watch as she reaches up and strokes her fingers over the plastic casing protecting the poster.

"You know, we always talked about coming here to see it. Together. But we never did. Too far away. Too hard to get to. Never enough time. Never enough money. I mean, it's only a sheet of paper. Who'd want to travel so far just to see a sheet of paper?"

I look around. The whole area seems shrouded in

shadow and mist. I can make out a couple of Winnebagos sitting in a nearby car park. Far off, I spot some people taking pictures of each other standing next to a few of the more interesting-looking rocks.

"You said that you thought Brindabel was here," I say to Tarni. "Can you see her?"

Tarni's gaze doesn't move from the poster.

"She's here," she says. "But I won't see her...unless she wants me to see her."

I look around the reserve again. "Why not? What do you mean?"

Tarni doesn't answer. She looks like every drop of energy inside has gone from her. It is not the Tarni I have come to know.

And it scares me.

"Tarni," I say. "I don't understand."

"The night before she left," she slowly explains. "The night before Yaye went...she and Ma had an argument. It wasn't over anything important... I can't even remember what it was about, that's how small it was. A tiny thing, like washing the dinner plates or something. I dunno. Something small which really shouldn't matter...

"Anyway...they argued...and Ma went to *her* bed angry and my sister went to *her* bed angry.

"And I went to *my* bed, angry with them both."

Her hand reaches up and wipes something from her cheek; and I realize that she's crying.

"Then...the next morning...she'd gone."

I keep quiet.

"Ma spent the whole day crying. *I* spent the whole day crying. There wasn't anything we could do. She'd just... gone."

Tarni taps her chest with her finger and turns to me. "There was something...there was something in her heart, you see... Something that had been there a *real* long time. Something...wrong. Probably been there since she was born...that was what they said."

I feel a sudden sickness in my stomach.

"Might always have been there. Always. When we were out climbing trees together...when we went fishing for yabbies...when we were laughing at some ridiculous thing. All that time, it was there. Growing. Getting bigger. Crawling across Yaye's heart."

Yaye.

I think of the word.

Yaye.

And then I realize just how blind I'd been all this time. How I'd only ever seen what I thought I'd seen. How I'd missed so much because I never really looked close enough to spot the truth.

Yaye.

Kwementyaye.

The substitute name used when someone dies.

"She's…dead?" I ask softly. Unbelievingly. "Brindabel's…dead?"

Tarni doesn't answer. She just carries on talking. "After my sister…went… After she left us…the doctors found it. Nobody knew it was there. Not even Br—" She stops herself from saying her sister's name. "Not even Yaye. It was almost invisible."

She pinches her finger and thumb together to show how small it was. "Nobody could see it. A tiny thing… like washing the dinner plates.

"But it was big enough to take her away the night that we were all angry with each other."

Tarni wipes her hand across her face, her eyes wet and sore.

"It didn't happen on another night when we were all happy with each other and joking and laughing. It didn't happen on a night when we had all sat round and told each other silly ghost stories and eaten sweets. Nah. It came and it took her when we were all sad and lonely and crying in our beds.

"And that's the worst thing of all. To know that my sister slipped out of her life and into the land of the dead when she was feeling sad and lonely and crying in her bed."

Tarni drops Candelabra's cage and her canvas bag and puts her face in her hands.

I am confused. I do not fully understand what is going on. But without saying anything, I throw the *Karpilowsky* to the ground, then stretch my arms round Tarni. I pull her to me and hug her as tightly as I possibly can, pressing my head to hers.

"Tarni," I whisper into her hair. "I didn't realize. I'm sorry."

I hold her and rock her gently from side to side for a long time. We don't say anything. There is no sound.

Only the almost silent thump of my heart against hers.

"But then…" she begins, in between soft sobs. I release her from my grip and step back so I can see her properly. "But then the nomad people came through Utopia. It was weeks after she went. Months. And some of them said they'd seen her…with Debonaire."

I suddenly remember something that Tarni had said the day she found me.

This land is full of spirits that walk across it.
Spirits.
Spirits walking.

"And I knew that if *they* could see her…then there was a chance I might be able to see her too. I wanted to tell her that…" She shakes her head. "Nah. The truth is…I just needed to see her again."

I reach out and take hold of her hands.

"You came here looking for your sister…" I say. "You travelled all the way across Australia to find her *spirit*?"

Tarni stares at the ground.

"But…what if she didn't go anywhere?" I continue. "What if she's always been with you… Around you… Watching over you? Guiding you."

Tarni nods and then looks right at me. "You felt it too?"

"I…I think I have," I stutter. "I don't understand it but…yes."

Tarni smiles at me and somehow everything seems just a tiny bit better.

"And if she's always been with you," I say, "I'm sure she knows that the arguments you had didn't matter."

"Yeah," Tarni agrees quietly.

"She knows that it was all the other stuff that mattered. All the things you did together. All the good times. All three of you. Those were the things that counted. Those were the things you would all remember."

For a moment, I think about Mum and Dad and me, and my chest hurts.

"Yeah," Tarni says. "But…but I was also worried. Worried about *me*." She looks ashamed.

"What do you mean?"

Tarni sighs like she doesn't really want to say. "My sister had been such a big part of my life. *All* my life. We did *everything* together. When she went…I was stuck. I didn't know who I was. I didn't know who I was supposed to be any more. I was confused. Such a big part of me had gone…so big that I wasn't sure what was left. So, I wanted to find her to…I dunno…ask her if I could be *me* again. Alone. Without her."

"Tarni," I say. "I never met your sister – and I couldn't *possibly* know you as well as *she* knew you. But I don't think she would ever want you to apologize for being you."

I look into Tarni's wet eyes.

"Look…I know that you relied on your sister, and that she relied on you. Like the two rocks balanced one on top of the other in your sketch.

"But I think…no…I *know*…that you are strong enough to be your own person too. To be an individual. I don't think you need your sister's permission to be you.

"Because I think you just…*are*.

"You."

The dark sky above us clears a little – a crack in the

clouds sending down a glorious, beaming strip of warmth over Karlu Karlu.

I squeeze Tarni's hands and she squeezes mine back.

"But...wait..." I say after a long while, several thousand thoughts suddenly hitting me at once. "There's something I don't understand. Debonaire... Your sister left a *letter* with Debonaire. And the *letter* at the hotel... How could she have left *letters* with them?"

Tarni reaches into the pocket on the front of her dungarees and pulls out some pieces of paper. The hotel letter. Debonaire's map. Some strips of the letter that Tarni ripped up. She holds them out to me in her hand.

I lean forward to take them from her.

And then...

Like bright sunlight dimming through a curtained window...

They fade.

They fade until I can almost see through them, and then...

They are gone.

Tarni's fingers are empty.

I hear my own cries in my throat and I stand there, unable to move. I think I must look stunned, because

Tarni smiles gently as if to reassure me.

"It's okay, Tidda. Don't worry. There's nothing to worry about."

"What's...what's happening, Tarni?" I squeak. "I don't understand." But my mind is skittering. "Wait! But if Debonaire *spoke* to your sister... If she *gave* you the letter..."

I reach round and pull the rucksack off my back, holding it out in front of me.

"Debonaire gave me this. If Debonaire gave you the letter, and then she gave me this..."

Suddenly, the weight of the strap on my fingers becomes nothing as the rucksack itself turns paler and paler until it – and everything inside it – fades completely into the air, like the paper.

I look down and I see that my feet are now bare and standing on the hot, dusty earth.

"My boots!" I cry. "The boots that she gave me..."

Tarni nods.

"Gone," she says.

I can't speak for a few moments. All I can do is steady myself and try to stay standing up.

This land is full of spirits that walk across it.

"Debonaire?" I say, taking deep breaths. "Debonaire... she wasn't...real? She was a...mirage? An angel? A spirit?"

Tarni nods again. "That's how my people would see it. There are probably loads of other ways. Depends on what you believe," she says.

"And the hotel...that wasn't real too, was it? Like the people in the car said. It was a...it was a..." I swat at the air trying to catch the right word. "It was a *ghost*? It wasn't real."

"Y'know, *real* is a strange word to use," says Tarni calmly. "Everything's *real*. It's just that some things are more real than others. Perhaps *I'm* more real than *you*. Perhaps *you're* more real than *me*. Just depends how you look at it all. Different people look at different things different ways."

"But the hotel...it wasn't there. Was it?" I persist. "Like your mum being interviewed on the television..."

Tarni smiles. "Okay. If that's how you want to think of it. No. The hotel wasn't there. Eddy. Debonaire. The receptionist. Perhaps other things too. Perhaps other people. Perhaps *none* of them were there."

"Eddy?" I howl. "Him too?"

Tarni laughs, and the sight of her laughing through her red eyes makes me want to laugh too, even though my thoughts are like a fog and I can barely remember my name again.

"Yes. Him too."

Spirits of ancestors that take care of the land and protect it and its people, Tarni had said all those days ago.

Protect it and its people.

"They were all spirits. Angels. Ghosts. Or…whatever," I falter. "They…were…protecting you?"

"Protecting *us*," Tarni stresses. "Both of us. In a way. Eddy helped us find water. Debonaire helped us recover from being poisoned. *All* of them tried to make me go back home."

"What about the Drongos?" I ask, but before Tarni has a chance to open her mouth, I think I answer my own question. "Yowies. Or something like that. Spirit monsters. Yes? Like you said, not all spirits are good. Hmm?"

Tarni stares at me saying nothing.

"And…" I struggle to find the words. "And…you *knew*? You *knew* they were all spirits?"

Tarni nods. "Kinda. In a way. I dunno. Yes."

"Why didn't…why didn't you tell me?"

"Well…I s'pose I was worried it might all be a bit… *mystical* for you. Thought you might not handle it very well." There is a spark in her eye. It is a spark that tells me that the old Tarni is still here. That she hasn't gone away just yet. That she is still just standing right in front of me.

"City-girl eyes," she says, pointing at me.

And somehow, despite my confusion and shock, I find myself laughing.

We walk our way over a rocky path that weaves itself like a rainbow snake across Karlu Karlu. My bare feet hardly notice the sharp and spiky stones that try to cut them – so hardened have my soles become.

Above us, the clouds in the sky have disappeared – like magic – and the heat has become its usual oppressive self once again. The fabric of my dress is sticking to my body like glue and my arms are wet with sweat.

"You know, you could have saved yourself a lot of bother if you'd just listened to the letter that your sister had left with Debonaire," I tease. "If you'd just turned around and gone back home."

"I s'pose. But if we hadn't come, I would never have seen all this…" She sweeps her free arm around at all the strangely beautiful rock formations that fill this alien-looking landscape. "And if we hadn't come, we would have never started the song."

She stops and turns back to me.

"The song," she says.

"Hmm?" I stop walking too.

She looks serious.

"The song."

"What about it?" I ask.

"I think it's time to finish it."

I shake my head. "Isn't there something else you need to do first?" I ask, looking down at Candelabra's cage. Inside I can see him strutting along his makeshift perch and tapping the bars of his cage with his beak. "Before we finish our song."

Tarni says nothing.

"Tarni..." I start.

"Yeah," replies Tarni with a sigh. "I know what you're going to say. I know."

I stand as Tarni drops her canvas bag and lifts up Candelabra's cage by the handle, holding it close to her face.

"Hey, mister," she says sadly. "Guess what...? It's time."

Alongside us is a long, flattish rock. With one free hand to help her, Tarni climbs to the top of it and plants her feet solidly, the cage swaying slightly.

I stay with my bare feet fixed on the ground, leaning against the side of the hot rock, looking up at her.

I feel like crying.

"So...Candelabra," Tarni says. "*Candelabra.* Such an

awesome name. Such a *deadly* name. I think that's the best name any creature on Earth has ever *ever* had. *Candelabra*. So deadly..."

Tarni steadies the cage in her grip.

"But...the thing is...I realize that Candelabra is *not* your name. I know that's *not* what your bird friends and your bird family called you. But I'll never know what your *real* name was, even if I live to be a billion years old and grow wings myself...

"So, I'll *always* think of you as Candelabra."

Tarni sighs.

"Anyway...*Candelabra*. You know...it's time you went. It's time you moved on. Now that you're stronger and can make the journey...you need to fly away. From me. Take your wings and use them. Fly on to where you need to be. To where you now belong. Fly your way across the sky and sing your song...sing it loud, so that everyone who has ever loved you can hear you and be reminded of you and be happy that you are flying again. Up in the sky. Make them all happy, little fella, like you made *me* happy."

I see the tears in Tarni's eyes.

"You know, I always knew you'd have to go," she says, her voice fraying. "I knew it wouldn't be right to hold on to you for ever – even though I wanted to. Wanted to keep you with me through all the good times, all the bad times and all the times in between. Wanted you by my side to tell all my hopes and my fears and my secrets to. Wanted you there to love and be loved by. Wanted you for ever.

"But…now I know…at least you were with me…for a while." Tarni looks down at me and can see that I am crying too. "For a time. And I am grateful for it. I am real grateful that you went along with me…if not for *all* the way…at least for *part* of the way." She wipes her nose with the back of her wrist. "I am pleased that I found you and helped you to be you again.

"But now…well…it's time."

Tarni reaches to the front of the cage and unlatches the string hook.

"Time for you to leave little bird…"

She opens the door to the cage.

"Time to fly."

I smile as Candelabra pokes his funny little head out of the opening – twitching one way and then the other, as if someone has just knocked on his front door and then run away – before disappearing back inside.

And then—

Swhooosh.

Candelabra launches himself out through the opening and up into the air. Like a rocket. Like a bullet. Like something you just wouldn't expect. We watch as he goes up, up, up towards the rich blue of the sky. So graceful. Twisting and flickering in the afternoon haze. No longer a drab, funny little thing with an orange beak and orange feet. No longer a cage-bound broken-winged bellbird with a skull-rattling cry.

No.

Now he is the same as the brightest of stars.

"Thank you!" shouts Tarni with a cracked voice.

Some honeyeaters join Candelabra as he circles directly above us for a few seconds, before one final swoop above our heads – like he is thanking *us* – and then a sudden flash in the sky…and he is gone.

"Thank you."

Tarni waves and, as I stare in the direction of Candelabra's flight, I can see a far-off shape waving back.

"I love you," whispers Tarni as the shape turns and disappears into a shimmering glow. "I always will."

A *mirage*, I tell myself.

Though I know that isn't true.

CHAPTER TWENTY-THREE

THE SONG

The song.

The song is like a tree.

It begins in the spark of a meteor shower, the ripple and rhythm of tide and wave, the pulse and surge of earth and root. Groping underground creatures carry the song between delicate satin paws, bringing it to light where melody changes form to leaf, bark, shoot.

Song, you are like a tree.

Spreading your arms open wide in supplication, embrace. Stars tremble through your canopy, sun dapples your shade, insects nestle in your whorls, leaves rustle in your dance. That you may ever dance, move still, still so. Birds alight on your palm, and then take flight, beaked with jewelled berries that drop like colourful rain on this desert plain.

Song, you are a tree.

Ships set sail in your lifetime, cities rise, empires fall but you know nothing of this and it doesn't matter. Standing tall, even as the wind-bridled horses drum and swerve the sand with sun-molten hooves, shake your dust. No tombstone, snow or lonely flower here.

Just you.

A fragile figure in silvery hue, your hands, tiny in all this air, applauding.

"This is our song," she says, "yours and mine."

"This is our song," I say, "until the end of time."

We walk slowly together through Karlu Karlu. Past the balancing rocks and the heavy-leafed gumtrees. Past the fat wheeled four-by-fours and silver Winnebagos. Past the sweating selfie-taking tourists and the cool uniformed park rangers.

And it is weird.

Everything and everyone is still.

Nothing and nobody moves.

There is no breeze.

There is no heat.

There is no noise.

No one notices us.

We are almost invisible.

Then something happens…

A door, seemingly sliced into the air, opens before us, and out from the brightness behind, into this landscape, steps a figure.

Madame Petrovsky.

She is wearing her long, black concert dress. Her hair is tied up into a neat bun and round her neck is an antique emerald necklace – the one she always keeps for the most special of performances.

"Detenysh," Madame Petrovsky says and stretches out her hand towards me. "It is time. Don't be late. Are you coming?"

I turn to look at Tarni and I can see that she has taken a step away from me.

"Tarni," I say. "What is happening?"

Tarni pulls her bag tighter over her shoulder and stares down at her feet.

"Tarni?"

And then realization gushes over me and I find myself dropping the violin case onto the dust to keep myself steady.

"Oh. I see," I say.

"I understand.

"At least, I *think* I understand."

I shake my head.

"I'm not here, am I?

"I'm not *really*...here right now."

I am struggling to put everything into words. Strange, unbelievable words.

"I'm a...I'm a spirit too...aren't I? Like your sister. Like the others. I'm a... spirit."

The stillness and the silence are smothering me almost as much as the heat ever did, as I try to thread my thoughts together.

"When...when the plane crashed...I escaped," I say. "I walked away. It said that in the paper, didn't it? That was true. But...but then...afterwards..."

I stop. I try to form even more unbelievable words. Try to shape them in my mouth and say them out loud.

"Did...did I die?"

Tarni shakes her head "No," she whispers. "I don't think so. Not yet."

I glance back at Madame Petrovsky, who still stands with her hand outstretched towards me.

"I don't understand," I say.

I look around. Everyone is fixed like statues. As still as the marbles themselves.

As I turn and look, I think about the young girl trapped in a glittering tower, staring down at the children playing below. I think about the hard work and discipline that dominates and shapes every single day of my life, leaving little room for anything else. I think about the tears of Figgy Day. I think about the nasty, spoilt, sarcastic girl without any friends who will do anything she can to be the best.

And then I think about my love of music. I think about standing on the stage of a world-famous concert hall and playing, and how joyful that makes me feel. I think about Violet Crumbles purring on my bed, clawing at the sheets. I think about the photograph of Mum and Dad holding on to each other, crying, at a press conference.

And I think about my friend Tarni and everything we've been through together.

And I know what I have to do.

"Madame…" I address my teacher. "Anastasia. Thank you. You tried to protect me in the plane as it started to drop out of the sky. I remember you holding onto me. You held onto my shoulders and told me to be brave.

"And I *have* been brave. Ever since then – ever since remembering – I have tried to be as brave as *you* were in those final moments.

"But now I have to be the bravest I could ever be.

"You see… I have to turn around.

"I am going to go back to wherever I really am right now, and I am going to be *me*. Not the old me. But a new version of me. Someone who cares about people and the way they feel. Someone who has control of their own life. Someone who will laugh and cry and play with others simply because they can. Because they want to. Someone who can play music with heart.

"All because of my friend, Tarni."

Madame Petrovsky nods and smiles. "Goodbye, Detenysh. We will meet again, one day." And she steps backwards into the bright doorway and the light of the sun fades it all away to nothing as it closes behind her.

"Goodbye, Anastasia," I whisper.

There remains the silence and stillness.

Only Tarni and I appear to breathe in this snapshot of the world that has wrapped itself around us. Not even the birds sing now.

I turn to Tarni.

"Tarni?" I ask. "Are you a spirit too?"

Tarni laughs. "No, Tidda. I'm not."

"How long have you known about…well…me?"

Tarni shakes her shoulders up and down. "I dunno. Don't think I *ever* knew. Think I *always* knew. I dunno." She smiles at me. "Spirit walker."

I think back to something Tarni said to me in the cave.

There are cultures all over the world that believe in spirit walking. It's when your spirit – or your soul – leaves your body for some reason and goes somewhere else. Goes travelling.

I smile back at her.

"You know, Tarni," I say. "I think it's time for us to go home now. Both of us. I think you should do what your sister asked you to do and return to your mother." I point to where a park ranger stands frozen next to a Parks Service truck. "When I go, you need to tell them who you are. Tell them where you've come from. Tell them to take you back to Utopia."

Tarni frowns. "Maybe I can go back with you? We can walk together. I can easily do it. You know that."

I shake my head. "No. I think I have to go back alone. I don't know how I know that but something tells me I have to go back alone. For me."

Tarni nods sadly. "I know."

We stand there not saying anything for a while, just looking at each other, thinking each other's thoughts.

Eventually I take the violin case by the handle and straighten myself up. "Okay..."

"Okay..." says Tarni back.

We stare into each other's eyes.

And then…

I nod my head at Tarni…

And Tarni nods her head at me.

Like Tarni's farewells with Eddy and Debonaire, there is no need to say anything more. Everything that needs to be said, we already both know.

So I smile, I turn and I start walking…

As I walk, the sun arcs in reverse across the sky, days sprinting backwards like minutes. The sky turns dark, then bright. Dark, then bright. Dark, then bright as I march my way along the route already taken…

…*thgir, tfel, thgir, tfel, thgir, tfel*…

I look behind me and see that I am not leaving any footprints…

Past the information board with Tarni's sketch…

Past the service road where the hotel once stood…

Past the dunes where we set the filly free…

Past the place where Tarni and I argued…

Past the wood where Debonaire's caravan never was…

Past the gas station where Tarni read the paper…

Past the dirt track where the Drongos tried to catch me…

Past the cave where I opened up the case…

Past the hill where Candelabra escaped...

Past the spot where we ate eggs with Eddy...

Past the watering hole where I spotted the plane...

Past the perfectly named Lookout Rock...

Past the ditch with the billygoat Plum tree...

To the place where Tarni found me...

And where I still am, as the spinning helicopters land about me.

And it is from this place and this moment in time that I walk my own song into the future.

STILL LIFE

Overture – 1 *Music* An orchestral piece at the
beginning of a musical work.
2 An introduction to something more substantial.
(*Oxford English Dictionary*)

The gallery owner is far too busy organizing the sparkling trays of champagne glasses to see her slip in through the door, silver violin case at her side.

Shaking off the heat of the late afternoon sun, Sienna Vanderbolt pours herself a small tumbler of iced water, props the *Karpilowsky* on a stiff wooden chair and wanders through the rooms, studying the pictures fixed to the walls.

She smiles to herself as she moves from one painting to another. Brushstrokes of bright, vital oranges are pitted against swirls of ominous blacks and greys. Languid sweeps of blue battle it out with jealous stabs of green. Blinding yellows and soothing pinks all fight for their place on these canvasses.

So vibrant.

So exciting.

So instantly recognizable.

She walks through to another room. Stark whitewash with harsh lights blaring down on one huge, rectangular painting that dominates the wall.

Taking a sip of the water, she stands directly in front of it and stares.

In the centre of the canvas is a limousine. Black and stretched. The sort that rich and famous people swoon about in. Inside, a driver in cap and uniform, his left hand reaching out to tune the radio.

In the back of the limousine, a woman with her hair in a bun, silvering at the top as if a handprint of tinkling stars has come to a gentle rest on top of her head. Her arm around the shoulders of a girl with hair the colour of straw and lemons, a thin straight mouth, her right hand resting on the case sitting between them, her left hand curled about a small object, possibly a sweet or a marble. Its colours seeping into the skin of her fingers so that it looks as if she's dipped her hand in cake sprinkles.

Behind the car is a woman in suit and heels, her hand held up as if in farewell, standing behind gates in front of a large white house, and in the bottom sash window of the large white house sits the silhouette of a fluffy cat.

A small red plane waits on standby in the right-hand corner of the painting, but Sienna's eye is not drawn to this.

Sienna's eye is drawn to something in the extreme top left-hand corner of the painting.

What can it be?

She leans in closer and squints.

A bird, tiny and iridescent, one wing stretching over

the edge of the canvas, the other glancing a sun that is rippling and golden, as if a million fireflies have been corralled into its orbit.

A bird.

Flying high and free, escaping the limits of the frame, the constraints of space and time.

Sienna puts the glass of water down on the floor, touches the small clear, straight scar on her cheek and swallows down the beginnings of a tear.

"You've seen it then?" A voice behind makes her spin round on her Mary Jane heels. "What do you think?"

Sienna looks back at the enormous painting before her.

"I think...it's brilliant."

Tarni comes alongside Sienna, her arms folded, staring up at her own creation. "Oh, I wouldn't go that far."

Sienna smiles. "Well, you should. I think it's...perfect."

Tarni gives a small, embarrassed shake of the shoulders. "Thanks, Tidda."

"What are you calling it? The painting?"

"It's called *Still Life*."

Sienna turns her head to look at Tarni. "*Still Life?*"

"Yep."

"Why *Still Life*? In still life paintings there are always apples or water jugs or ladderback chairs, aren't there?

353

Vases of flowers. Half-drunk cups of coffee. That kind of thing." Sienna points to the painting. "I can't see any of those."

The artist smiles. "I know. But whatever happens… whatever things occur…well…there's *always* life. There's *still* life. No matter what."

Sienna nods. "How come you are always so wise?"

"Dunno, Tidda. I think some of us are just lucky enough to be born that way." She winks at Sienna. "Anyway, art should mean something. Otherwise there's no point in doing it."

They stand there in silence for a while, watching the dried gouache catch the light.

"First major Melbourne art exhibition, eh?" says Sienna eventually. "That's pretty impressive."

"Transfers to New York at the end of the month." Tarni tries not to swagger.

"Woah! Really? New York? That's amazing! Congratulations!"

Tarni struggles to hide her grin. "Thanks, Tidda. Maybe I can visit you when I'm over there?"

"*Stay* with me. It'll be fun. I'll show you the sights."

"Deadly!"

Tarni lowers her arms, and the two young women slip their hands into one another's.

"Your mum's coming tonight, isn't she?" asks Sienna.

"Oh yeah," replies Tarni. "Couldn't keep her away. I *tried* – trust me – but she insisted."

"Good. Be nice to see her again."

"Ah! Ms Vanderbolt! I hadn't realized you had arrived. Delighted to meet you at long last!" The gallery owner struts into the room, takes Sienna's hand and shakes it eagerly. "So very pleased. I am *such* a fan of your music. Such a fan. I listen to your album all the time when I'm driving in the car." He drops her hand as quickly as he took it. "It's so generous of you to give up your time like this. So very kind."

"Yes, well, Tarni and I are good friends. She's such a brilliant artist."

"She is. She is." The man smiles at Tarni. "An incredible Alyawarre talent. So original. We're very lucky to be staging her exhibition." The man points towards the door. "May I show you where you'll be performing? Doors open in less than an hour and you might wish to warm up. We're expecting quite a crowd."

The gallery owner leads the way out of the room into a slightly bigger, rather darker space. Sienna and Tarni follow.

"You're looking very snazzy," Sienna says to Tarni, pointing to the flowery summer dress she is wearing.

355

"You know, I don't think I've ever seen you in a dress before."

Tarni frowns. "And I don't think you'll ever see me in one again, Tidda. I feel like a stuffed emu." She tugs at the collar. "I think next time I'll just stick on my dungarees and T-shirt."

The gallery owner indicates a small, raised stage in the corner of the exhibition room.

"I hope this is okay for you, Ms Vanderbolt. I realize you're used to playing larger venues. But hopefully this will feel...well, intimate."

Sienna steps up onto the stage. "It's perfect," she says, as Tarni steps up next to her. "Anyway, I'm just the accompanist. The background musician. Tarni's art is the star."

Tarni snorts. "Yeah whatever, Tidda, you daft galah!"

The gallery owner looks up at them both like he doesn't quite know how to join in with their conversation.

"I'll...leave you both to it. Please, if there's anything you need, just ask." He quickly spins and marches out of the room, leaving the two young women on their own.

"I think he's a bit nervous. Opening night and all that," says Tarni. "Thinks he's going to spill champagne all over the mayor or something. Canapés down a councillor's shirt. I suppose you've got your good luck charm with you?"

"Always."

Sienna nods and reaches into a pocket on the front of her silky, black dress and pulls out something round.

She holds it out to Tarni who takes it and rolls it around in her hand.

"Ha! Been a long time since I've seen this." She holds the stone up to the light and runs her finger over the shape of the horse she painted there some years ago. "Whatever happened to your giant green marble?" she asks. "The one you won off…" She struggles to remember the name.

"Figgy Day," adds Sienna. "Oh, I gave it back to her. It didn't really belong to me. It was hers. And, anyway, I think this one carries much more positive energy. It brings me more luck."

Tarni hands the stone back and Sienna slips it into her pocket before retrieving the *Karpilowsky* from the other room.

"So," Sienna says, pulling the violin out of its case, "for most of the evening I'll be in the background. Just accompanying your show. Unobtrusive. I'll play some Bach, Mendelssohn, a few of my own compositions. But at the end…"

"Yeah," says Tarni, nodding and smiling widely. "I'm looking forward to this. I've been practising all week."

Sienna smiles back. "Me too."

"The Song Walker."

"Hmm. *Our* walking song. You can remember it?"

Tarni makes a face as if to say *you're kidding* and Sienna laughs.

"Okay," says Sienna. "Perhaps we should run through it."

"Yeah. Just a couple of times, Tidda. Just to make sure you're in the right key!" Tarni winks once again.

Putting the violin to her chin, Sienna takes up a position to the side of the stage, and Tarni stands in the middle.

"Okay?"

"Okay."

"Then I'll count us in. Ready?

"One,

"Two,

"Three,

"Four!"

And the tiny iridescent bird peels away from the painting, flies over the darkened stage, out of the window and into the sun. Each and every feather illumined in that final grace of light.

The journey completed and only just begun.

ACKNOWLEDGEMENTS

To the star people who have supported me and
my work over the years, I owe you a huge debt of
gratitude. Wishing you all good health, peaceful
sleep, many joys and infinite love.

AUTHOR'S NOTES

The Songlines

As a child growing up in Papua New Guinea, I learnt about the songlines. I particularly liked how the melody and rhythm of the songs seemed to follow the contours of the land they passed over because it felt as if the land were being sung into existence; that the song created the land as much as the land created the song. The beauty and power of this idea seemed immeasurable to me as a child and it still does.

The Karpilowsky

Stradivarius violins are each ascribed a unique nickname. The Karpilowsky is a real violin and was actually stolen from the Los Angeles home of Hollywood musician Harry Solloway in March 1953. In truth, the Karpilowsky has never been found.

BOOK CLUB QUESTIONS

1. The first chapter of the story is called The End. Did that surprise you? Why do you think the author called it this.

2. Suffering from memory loss must be a very frightening and disorienting experience. Can you imagine how you might feel if you were to wake up with no clue as to who you are or what you're doing in a particular place. How do you think other people might react towards you?

3. Many people think names are an important part of who we are. Why do you think Tarni keeps changing the name she gives Sienna? Which name do you think suits her best?

4. When the girls first meet Sienna is reliant on Tarni for her survival but gradually we see that Tarni also needs Sienna. Do you think there is a particular moment when we see that switch?

5. The Australian Outback is a beautiful but very hostile place. Which words or phrases does the author use to give you a sense of this incredible landscape?

6. Tarni gets cross with Sienna and says she doesn't understand much. Why do you think Tarni finds it so hard to tell Sienna what's really going on?

7. Why do you think Tarni keeps Candelabra in the cage? What do you think the bird represents and why do you think Tarni lets it go when she does?

8. Do you think Sienna liked her previous life? How do you think her violin playing might change after her experiences in the outback?

9. Why do you think Tarni is so sad that what happens to her sister takes place after an argument?

10. Were you surprised by what you learnt about the characters at the end of the story? Looking back do you think the author gave us hints and clues along the way?